Irish
Rose

Jacqueline Marten

Books by Jacqueline Marten

English Rose
Irish Rose

Published by TAPESTRY BOOKS

An *Original* publication of TAPESTRY BOOKS

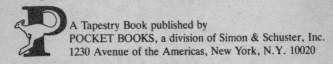

A Tapestry Book published by
POCKET BOOKS, a division of Simon & Schuster, Inc.
1230 Avenue of the Americas, New York, N.Y. 10020

ISBN: 0-671-50722-2

First Tapestry Books printing April, 1984

10 9 8 7 6 5 4 3 2 1

POCKET and colophon are registered trademarks
of Simon & Schuster, Inc.

TAPESTRY is a trademark of Simon & Schuster, Inc.

Printed in the U.S.A.

To
The Jane Austen Society of North America,
particularly those charter members
who gathered together at
Gramercy Park, October 1979,
and to Albert,
who learned I was not the only
Janeite weirdo in town.

ACKNOWLEDGMENTS

To Miss Jane Austen of Steventon and Chawton, England, author of six gems in the English language: *Sense and Sensibility, Pride and Prejudice, Mansfield Park, Emma, Northanger Abbey*, and—with particular gratitude in the case of *Irish Rose—Persuasion*.

And to my cousin, Edward Neustadt, who started my library and brought the first copy of Jane Austen into my home.

Prologue

STEPPING QUICKLY AND QUIETLY, A YOUNG man emerged from the drawing room, shutting the doors firmly against a loud babble of voices and more distant strains of music.

"Whew!" he whistled soundlessly, loosening the top button of his jacket collar and then carefully removing an infinitesimal speck of lint from just above the lieutenant's insignia of his spanking new naval uniform.

A butler appeared in the great hallway and had gotten no farther than a questioning "Sir?" when the young man put one finger to his lips and waved him off.

Smiling his understanding, the butler backed away.

The lieutenant had gone just three steps up the curved, thick-carpeted stairway when a voice sounded close behind him.

"David Fenton! Just where do you think you are going?"

She was just behind him, hands on hips, her crinoline still swaying from her calculated stealthy approach.

"Out to the gardens for a breath of air?" he suggested feebly.

"The nearest approach to the gardens," a governessy voice informed him, "is back where you came from, and it has been raining these last two hours."

He eyed the frescoed ceiling for inspiration, then offered, "I suddenly got the urge for a game of cards?"

"Oh, indeed!" A disdainful sniff. "It's news to me that Papa moved the card room upstairs in the last few hours. Would you like to try again, David?" she inquired sweetly.

He looked squarely into the sparkling dark eyes so like his own. "There are reasons— unmentioned in polite society—why one withdraws from a group of people. I do not wish to offend your delicate sensibilities, *dear* Cousin Eleanor, but . . ."

"Stuff!" said his dear cousin Eleanor forthrightly. "I have no delicate sensibilities, and neither do you. *That* much I do remember from the many holidays we spent together. The truth is, you were making your escape. Don't try to deny it, Davey."

"I won't," he promised meekly.

"Fine conduct for a new-made officer and

supposed-to-be a gentleman, Lieutenant Fenton."

"Guilty as charged," he admitted, "but show me some compassion, sweet coz. It has been a long day of travel to get here. I looked forward to a comfortable family dinner, some friendly gossip with you, and some equally friendly political argument with Uncle and Tom over our port. What do I get? A full-dress company meal, followed, God help me, by some musical—for want of another word to describe it—entertainment and then an impromptu dance. I considered I had done my duty gallantly."

"You slighted some of the ladies you should have asked to dance."

"Impossible. Your mother and your charming neighbor, Lady Caroline Rosellen, were kind enough to refuse me. I partnered Lady Caroline's eldest daughter. I forget her name . . ."

"Catherine," murmured his cousin. "She is usually considered far from forgettable."

"So she might be," Lieutenant Fenton admitted, "if one were willing to accept beauty without animation. Miss Rosellen was all complaisance when first I asked her to stand up with me. After all, I'm a visiting nephew of the Earl of Denby. Who knew, especially a young lady on the catch for a husband, what

3

magic rank and fortune might not be masked by a lieutenant's humble uniform?"

"Ah, poor Davey, did you tell her?"

"I had no choice, my dear. Before we had circled the room a full two times, a half-dozen ruthless questions, which I could not avoid answering without a rudeness to match her own, had given Miss Catherine all the information she sought. I had neither rank nor fortune, and only my uncle's extreme good will but little influence with the admiralty to help me higher in the world. The lady was quite obviously reminding herself that Uncle William and your two deplorably healthy brothers, one married, stood between me and the earldom. After that, I might as well have been holding a corpse in my arms, an amazingly beautiful one, but nevertheless a corpse."

"While it is true," Lady Eleanor admitted judiciously, "that Catherine is a snob and mercenary as well, I cannot see any sailor in Her Majesty's Navy—particularly *you*, David —being so easily set down by a debutante's snub."

"I was not," David protested. "With my flags still flying, I next engaged the haughty beauty's sister."

"At least you could never call Margaret cold."

"No, indeed," he agreed cordially. "A delectable armful—spun-gold hair, sky-blue eyes, and the most grating giggle it has ever been my misfortune to have constantly dinned into my ears. If her sister had nothing to say, then Miss Margaret had far too much, and most of it was utterly without sense. Ignorance—even amiable ignorance—has no appeal for me."

Lady Eleanor snickered briefly, then tried once more to look and act severe. "If you are always to be so nice in your notions, Cousin, you will never get yourself a wife."

"At three-and-twenty, with my fortune yet to make, the bleak prospect does not wholly overwhelm me."

"You seemed to enjoy your dance with Mrs. Proudfoot."

"Had you nothing to occupy you but keeping track of my partners?" he demanded in some exasperation. "I did enjoy my dance with Mrs. Proudfoot so far as dancing was concerned. I was not even averse to the gentle flirtation she seems to demand of all her partners. I merely object to the use she makes of her fan while she flirts. Every time she uttered, 'Oh, you shameless flatterer'—and she declared me to be one at least four or five times—she slapped my left cheek with her folded fan. I am sure you can see a little redness there if you study it." He raised his cheek for her inspection. "It still feels bruised."

Giggling more like Margaret than herself,

Lady Eleanor rubbed his cheek with gentle fingers, forgot she was supposed to be annoyed with him, and said hilariously, "Harry swore to me that at our betrothal dinner Mrs. P. nearly knocked out one of his teeth with a swing of her fan."

Then she pursed her lips and eyed him sternly. "So, sir. My understanding of the situation is that, having been snubbed by Catherine, bored by Margaret, and slapped by Mrs. Proudfoot, you felt yourself entitled to withdraw without regard for the one lady left who might have expected a dance with you?"

"Precisely. Except that I felt I had done my duty by all the la—." He broke off, his eyes widening in horror. "Surely you don't mean that plump little dumpling of a girl with her hair sticking out like a fox brush—and of the same red color, I might add."

"Miss Janet Rosellen."

"Good God! A third daughter. Poor Lady Caroline. What an affliction!"

"Much you know. Jenny is the nicest of the lot."

"If by *nice* you mean *agreeable*, perhaps she may be. But aside from her unfortunate appearance, I watched that nicest girl trip over her petticoat in this very hallway when she entered the house, drop her napkin at least twice in the dining room, and break one

6

of your mother's favorite tea cups in the drawing room. You could not be so cruel as to ask me to subject my toes to the tender mercies of that particular damsel?"

"The particular damsel I had in mind, sir," she told him tartly, "was myself. But I can see how it is. You would rather go up to your bed."

He grinned ruefully. "Much rather. For this one night, at least. Forgive me, Nell." He leaned forward to kiss the tip of her nose.

"Go then, you shameless man," she mimicked and lightly slapped his left cheek, then pulled his head down to her and kissed it.

"Oh, David!" as he started up the stairs.

"Yes, my lady?"

"Jenny doesn't dance. She isn't out yet. But if she were, I doubt that she would accept *you* for a partner. She asked me once if it wasn't a terrible waste of time dancing an evening away with men, nine out of ten of whom had nothing to say worth hearing."

"And what did you answer?"

"I told her there was physical pleasure in the dancing itself, and one could always close one's eyes and block out the worst idiocies."

He laughed appreciatively. "Was that an acceptable alternative?"

"She was greatly impressed and so very eager to taste the experience that, knowing Jenny, I warned her off commanding their coachman to dance with her the next day. She is now resigned to allowing the situation to arise naturally."

"Good for Jenny, but I still say I would rather not be the first man she honors by stepping on his toes."

"Oh, go away," said Lady Eleanor crossly, and she left him standing on the stairs while she marched over to the drawing room doors. As the butler once more appeared to throw them open for her, she turned, as he had known she would, her smile warm and loving. "It's good to have you back, Davey. We missed you."

"It's good to be back."

He was smiling himself as he bounded up the stairs two steps at a time, but the smile froze on his face when he rounded the curve, out of sight of the lower hallway, and reached the head of the stairway.

A girl was sitting on the top step, a plump girl with fox-red hair broken loose from its tiny encircling garland of flowers and sticking out more than ever like a fox brush. She was balancing a well-filled plate on her lap and holding a champagne glass in her hand, while two demurely crossed ankles, instead of preserving her modesty as she no doubt thought, gave unexpected leverage to her hoop, providing the viewer several steps below with a

comprehensive glimpse of lace-edged petticoats and beribboned pantaloons.

Lieutenant Fenton looked down at the hallway and was forced to accept that there was
no possibility that Miss Janet Rosellen had
missed a single word of his exchange with
Lady Eleanor. Under the circumstances, he
could not but admire her perfect composure.
She glanced casually up at him, then went on
eating with every appearance of good appetite.

He stood before her awkwardly. "I am
afraid I owe you an apology."

"I don't see why." She dipped a succulent
shrimp into some sauce and nibbled at it
thoughtfully. "You were not to know that I
was by. I *was* quite angry at first. Then I
reflected that you were holding a private conversation with your cousin in her father's
house, so what right had I to object to your
expressing any opinions that you held?"

She drank the remainder of her champagne
as though it were water, eyeing him over the
rim of the glass. "You were rather unkind, of
course," she pointed out, "but then I have
noticed, haven't you, it's ever so much easier
to be witty when saying unkind things about
someone rather than something pleasant?"

"Is this little chit trying to put me to the
blush?" he asked himself, half amused, half

angry. The sudden heated reddening of his cheeks told him that, if so, she had succeeded all too well.

"I haven't previously given it much thought. I am afraid you may be right."

"Oh, I know I am," returned the amazing child as she attacked another fat shrimp. "My fa—one of the stupidest men I know," she went on with her mouth full, "sounds almost clever when he gets satiric."

"Just the same," he said as he sat down on the step just below her, stretching out his long legs, "I do feel that I owe you a profound apology."

"If it makes you feel any better, I accept it." She shrugged. "If it would help assuage your guilt, however, allow me to tell you that I don't think any better of you than you do of me. Nell—Lady Eleanor—was quite right. If I did know how to dance—I shall have lessons this next winter—I would not consent to dance with *you*. If it is as much a pleasure as Nell says, I would like to share it with someone I really like."

"Miss Janet Rosellen," he said with playful solemnity, "you have now assuaged my feelings of guilt completely. I do not know when I have ever been more artlessly or more thoroughly snubbed."

"Truly?" Her face lit up as though he had paid her a fine compliment. He began to notice that, though it was too rounded a face for true beauty like her sister Catherine's, her eyes were the blue-green color he had studied many an afternoon at sea, changeable as the winds and tides, taking luster from the sun and dark mystery from sudden storms. True, there were more freckles across the bridge of her nose and the upper part of her cheeks than were acceptable in polite society, but still her skin had a strange translucent radiance. It reminded him of the pink pearls he had bought in the South Seas. He had a chamois-skin bag full of them, which traveled everywhere with him in his footlocker. When he found that mythical "nice" wife of his, then he intended to have them strung.

"I suppose," she said thoughtfully, "you are accustomed to people liking you because you are such a handsome man."

"No one has ever told me so before," he said gravely, conscious of an unexpected and absurd feeling of gratification.

"Oh, my, yes, you are." She studied the length of his outstretched legs and the breadth of his uniformed shoulders, the frank and open sun-browned face, the dark eyes full of laughter, just like Lady Eleanor's, and the crisp light-brown hair combed neatly to one side that curled up over the ears. "Of course, the uniform helps. It always does. The son of one of our tenants was positively ugly till he joined the army . . . but in his scarlet regimentals, oh my! All the girls fell a little in love with him."

"You too?"

"N-no, but I was only twelve," she explained. "That's a bit too young to fall seriously in love, I think."

"How old are you now, Miss Janet, if you don't object to my asking?"

"I don't object," she told him with her quaint little air of dignity. "I am almost half past fifteen."

He reached for her empty champagne glass and set it on the step beside her.

"I should like to say something to you, Miss Janet, and I hope you will believe I mean it from my heart. I have changed my mind about your appearance. I find it extraordinarily—pleasing."

"You mean I am not a plump little dumpling?" she said with the ghost of a smile.

"It would be dishonest to describe you as willowy," he said with an answering smile, "but I find on closer inspection your figure is right for you. Your complexion is glowing and, though I think you might find a more attractive style of wearing it, your foxfire hair is, well, vibrant."

His hand reached out to stroke gently the scrubby brush while she stared up at him in open-mouthed astonishment. "It's like silk," he said. Then his thumbs rubbed lightly down her cheeks. "And these are like velvet. Your eyes are—bewitching," he went on, watching them deepen, darken, and grow wide with shock. "They will one day capture a man's soul, not just his heart. My perspicacious cousin was right. You may never have your sister Catherine's perfection of features or your sister Margaret's very ordinary prettiness, but even now you outshine them both."

"What's perspi—p—th-that word?" she stammered.

"All-knowing."

"Oh, my!" she whispered.

"The next time I return here on leave, you will probably have had your coming out. In which case, Miss Rosellen, ma'am . . ." He detached the fingers of her right hand from the fork to which they clung and lifted her hand to his mouth. "In which case, dear Miss Janet," he continued, after his lips brushed fleetingly across her knuckles, "I entreat the honor of the first waltz with you and the privilege of taking you to supper."

He looked up from this brief caress to see her cheeks even more pinkly luminous than his pearls. "B-but what about your t-toes?" she stammered breathlessly.

"I have changed my mind about that, too, as I hope you have changed yours about dancing with me. I feel sure you will be light as thistledown in my arms and graceful as a fairy queen."

"I will dance with you, sir," she said softly.

Then, to his surprise and horror, her wonderful eyes slowly filled up with tears, which spilled over and started tumbling down her cheeks.

"My dear girl." He took her plate and laid it on the step beside the empty champagne glass, started to put an arm around her, and then thought better of it. Instead, he took her hand again, trying to comfort her distress.

"No, no." She shook her head, dashed the last of her tears away, her eyes bluer and greener and more shining than ever. "Pray don't be upset, sir, when *I* feel wonderful."

"Do you always cry when you feel wonderful?" he asked ruefully.

The crescendo of her laughter, especially when contrasted to Miss Margaret's teeth-gritting giggle, was a delightful sound.

"It was knowing that I will be light as thistledown in y-your arms," she told him, looking away over his shoulder, "and graceful as—graceful, the way you said."

He smiled at her like a benevolent uncle. "You *know* that you will be?" he asked indulgently.

A shadow of disappointment crossed her face. "Of course," she said simply, "if that's

14

what you expect me to be. Don't most people fulfill your expectations about them?"

Before he could answer the question, she offered her own earnest explanation. "If I knew you were dancing with me, expecting to have your toes trod on, then as surely as night follows day, that's what would happen. I would be so nervous, so busy trying to avoid being awkward, I inevitably would be." She studied his face seriously. "Haven't you ever found this to be so?"

"Perhaps girls are more sensitive," he began hesitantly, at which she made an abrupt, angry gesture of impatience. He had the strange notion that he had disappointed her again.

A sudden remembrance, forgotten these many years, flickered across his mind.

"By God!" he said abruptly. "Old Saunders."

"Old Saunders?"

"My first Latin master when I went away to school. A right proper bas—," he began reminiscently, then checked himself, but not before he saw by the betraying quiver of her lips that she was aware of the missing syllable.

He coughed. "A right proper beast," he said severely, as though she, not he, had been guilty of the impropriety.

He recalled and was telling her how when

Old Saunders called on him to translate, the schoolmaster would first deliver a tirade on his stupidity, his usual unpreparedness, and the little likelihood that young Fenton knew what he was about. By the time the hapless student got around to declining, he would stutter and stammer and wind up making all manner of mistakes in a passage he had known perfectly well at the start of class.

"Is that what you meant, Miss Janet?" he asked her.

"Yes," she sighed. "It's exactly what I meant."

"You are quite right, then, and I am sorry if I appeared to patronize you. Treated as though they will, people often do fulfill one's worst expectations. How did you get to be so wise, Miss Janet, at just half past fifteen?"

"My mother and I talk a great deal when we are alone together. About people and life and the world, not just silly things like fashions and servants and how many horrible embroidered pen wipers or silk flowers to supply the vicar for the Jews' basket. But mostly," she added thoughtfully, "it's my father."

"He talks to you, too?"

"Talks to me? My *father!*" She laughed incredulously. David noted it was not such a happy sound as it had been before. "Goodness me, no. He doesn't even like to *look* at me if he can help it." She crossed her hands in her lap, obviously quoting. "He thinks I am gauche and clumsy and unappealing. In public he always watches me, expecting me to prove him right." She spread her palms out, shrugging, her mouth twisted in a strange little moue. "So I usually do. Like tonight. Well, you saw me yourself," she reminded him defensively, "tripping down there in the hallway— and it was over my hoop, not my petticoat— dropping my napkin, breaking Lady Carroll's lovely tea cup." Her face crumpled a little. "She's so fond of those cups. Papa will never let me hear the end of it. And he will nag poor Mama for days, saying I am not fit to be let loose in decent company yet. The only reason he allowed me to come tonight was that Nell made such a point of it, and Mama persuaded him against his better judgment. It would have been wiser for me to stay at home."

"I cannot agree," he said gently. "If you had stayed at home, we would not have met. I cannot at the moment think of anything I would regret more than not meeting you tonight."

"Oh, my!"

He smiled slightly at the already familiar repetition. The breathless joy of those two words and the shining depths of her eyes conveyed more warmth and feeling to him than any young lady had ever expressed with multitudes of gushing phrases.

"Perhaps you do your father an injustice," he suggested after a moment's quite comfortable silence. "He may be only trying to correct faults that he feels will handicap you outside your family circle. I remember a time when Nell used to complain bitterly of her father's tyranny, and I assure you there never was a father more loving, more kindly, or more concerned than my uncle."

"Oh, I know that, and Nell did, too, even when she said it. But, you see . . ." She studied the pattern of her green and white striped crinoline skirt, wrapping herself once more in that quaintly mature mantle of dignity. "The circumstances are not the same. Lord William loves Nell. He *dotes* on her," she added wistfully. "Sir Lewis—my father—well, it's different with him. I am the big disappointment of his life. Every time he looks at me, he is reminded of it."

"My dear girl!"

"I was supposed to be a boy, you see."

"But, Miss Janet," he expostulated, "you have two older sisters. Is he equally disappointed in them?"

"Oh, no, but that's different. You see, Catherine was born in January ten months after Mama and Papa were married, and she looks just like him and all the Rosellens in the family portraits—dark and handsome and

18

full-figured and proud-looking. Then Margaret was born in December of the same year, and he always said she was the prettiest baby that ever was and the image of his mother, my grandmother Rosellen, who died last year and left Margaret her jointure. Besides, I once heard Penny say—Miss Penniston, our governess—"

She looked at him doubtfully. "I think it would probably be terribly improper to tell you what she said?"

He heard the questioning note in her voice. "I am a very safe repository for secrets," he assured her promptly. "As for proper, a sailor, you know, leads a very different life from the generality of men. The usual social restrictions do not apply to him," he managed to finish with unsmiling solemnity, on fire to know what Penny had said to make Miss Jenny Rosellen's cheeks so fiery red in remembrance. "Nothing you could say to me would ever be improper."

"Well, Penny was talking to our housekeeper, about me and my sisters, you know, and the way Sir Lewis was with us, comparing, you understand—"

She hesitated, and he pressed her nearer hand. "I understand, Miss Janet."

"Well, Penny said," she gasped out on a single long breath, "that Sir Lewis was so proud of his pr-prowess at st-stud, he readily forgave Mama that the first two were girls."

There was a short stunned silence before she added uncertainly, "I dare say, you understand, being a sailor, what that means?"

"Yes, Miss Janet," he said, tight-lipped. "I understand. Did you?"

"Well, yes." She wriggled uncomfortably, moving farther back against the balustrade. "From the horses and—and—well, I understood."

"It should not have been discussed either in your presence *or* your absence," the lieutenant said, subduing his surge of anger toward those who obviously did not make her well-being of great concern. "Since it was, however, cannot you accept that your father was just as reconciled the third time to having a daughter?"

"N-no." She had turned slightly away from him and was tracing the intricate carved design of the balustrade with her fingertips. "The situation was different by then. Mama had m-miscarried of t-two other children, and then my brother was born. Poor little darling, he only lived three weeks. A year later I came along, and being a girl was a double disaster because the surgeon said Mama could not have any more babies. Papa was so angry he would not visit her for a full week, and I was fostered out to one of our farm tenants till I was four years old. Mama used to visit me every day, but I hardly knew Sir Lewis—my father."

She slowly turned her head toward him, knowing with that uncanny instinct of hers that his speechlessness rose from fury and indignation, neither of which was directed toward her.

"Oh, I liked it." For the first time she took the initiative, touching his hands. "Truly, I was very happy with the Ramsays. They were both so good to me, and the children were such fun, John and Maude and Eddy—Eddy's gone to be a sailor, too, you know. You must watch for him if he ever gets on one of your ships and be very good to him—for my sake," she added shyly.

"I shall look for Eddy Ramsay and be very good to him—for your sake—if he gets on my ship."

"Thank you."

"You are more than welcome."

There was another short silence, then a warm confiding hand was slipped into his. "You must not blame Papa too much," said a small voice, and he looked at her in astonishment at this further piece of mind reading. He had been doing exactly that.

"He is the twelfth baronet in the direct

line," she explained. "He feels dreadfully humiliated that it dies out with him."

"The baronetcy?"

"Oh, no. The direct continuity. There's a lots-removed cousin, Henry Rosellen, the great-grandson of the eighth Sir Lewis, or maybe . . ." Her nose wrinkled up, and she started counting on her fingers. "Maybe it was the ninth. He'll inherit next."

"Then your father has no grounds for complaint," he told her shortly.

"One would think so, but men . . ." Her voice trailed off uncertainly. "And then there's my hair," she added hastily.

"What's wrong with it?" demanded her fierce new champion, forgetting his own description of her fox brush not half an hour past.

She smiled a secret smile to herself and did not remind him.

"It's red," she said.

"Red and beautiful."

Inwardly hugging herself with delight, she made a wry face. "Papa says 'red and Irish.'"

"I gather your father's, er, aversions include the Irish?"

"Well, he didn't like Grandfer Conroy, that's for sure. Sir Lewis says that it's no great thing to be an Irish Earl." Her lilting voice unconsciously took on the pompous note he had noticed in her father's pronouncements at the dinner table. "'He has more manure on his boots and hay in his hair than an ordinary English farmer.'"

"So your mother, Lady Caroline, is Irish?"

"Half. Her mother was English." She proceeded to tell him in great detail about the spirited English girl who had fallen in love with the Irish earl at her coming-out ball and eloped with him a month later, living happily ever after till her death two years ago.

"It was so romantic," she finished, sighing ecstatically. "My mother looks just like her. *My* looks come from the Conroys."

"I suspect that's only partly true. Your looks come from Miss Janet Rosellen, a very unique young lady. My dear girl, why are you crying now?"

"B-because less than an hour ago, you were d-despising me and—and I was h-hating you, and now we're sitting here, fr-fr-friends."

"Yes, Miss Janet, we're friends. Speaking of which, just why *are* you sitting here?"

She blushed guiltily and hung her head.

"Friends," he reminded her.

"I came here to eat," she said in a low, embarrassed voice.

"To eat?"

"I just *love* to eat," she confessed shamedly, "and Lady Carroll's suppers are famous throughout the county. Papa thinks such elaborate meals are vulgar and ostentatious." Her voice took on its quoting cadence. "But the food always sounded wonderful to me when Catherine and Margaret described it. Papa warned me I wasn't to have anything more than a little fruit salad and some lemonade. He says I have to lose some f-fat or I'll never g-get a husband, being st-stout," she hiccupped, "as well as my other handicaps. So I waited till he went into the card room. Then I knew he would be gone for hours."

Lieutenant David Fenton suppressed a mighty oath and an impossible dream to have Sir Lewis Rosellen, twelfth baronet in the direct line, under him as an ordinary seaman for one wonderfully revengeful half-hour.

"In that case you might have eaten in the supper room," he told her casually.

"Well, there's Catherine and Margaret." She looked at him out of the corner of her eye. "They might forget and mention it. Accidentally, of course."

"Of course."

"But mostly," she admitted honestly, "there's Mama. It would be unfair to her. For her to suspect I disobeyed him is one thing. To deliberately do it in front of her puts her in a difficult position."

"In other words, a matter of honor."

Her face lit up in that extraordinary way that gave brilliance to her eyes and beauty to her being.

"Yes, honor and conscience. Besides," she made a clean breast of it, "I wanted so badly to try some champagne. Even Mama would draw the line at champagne."

He laughed and twitched at a hanging strand of her foxfire hair. "I am glad you are not too much of an angel, Miss Janet. And I hope the champagne was worth tomorrow's headache."

"I won't know until tomorrow," she told him practically, then threw her arms over her head and rocked back and forth. "It was so cool going down," she murmured, "just like I was turned inside out. I felt all marvelous and free."

Free to talk a great deal more than she was accustomed to, he suspected, and he hoped she would not regret *that* either in the morning when her head hammered and her stomach heaved.

"Is the music getting louder, or is that the champagne, too?" Jenny asked dreamily after a while.

"No, it's definitely music. I think they have opened the doors."

"It's a waltz." Eyes closed, her body swayed so perilously in time to the music, it took his arm to keep her on the top step. She was in imminent danger of tumbling down the whole flight of stairs.

"May I have the honor of this dance, Miss Rosellen?"

Her eyes flew open. Her lips trembled. "I c-can't." It was almost a cry of pain. "I haven't had my lessons yet."

"I'll teach you, Miss Janet." He drew her up from the step and into his arms. "It's very easy to teach someone who is light as thistledown and graceful as a fairy queen."

He was right.

In no time at all they were whirling round and round together, hands clasped, her radiant face lifted flowerlike to his, her heart beating wildly against his jacket buttons. The taffeta-covered crinoline whipped behind her, permitting their legs to touch.

The music stopped, the waltz was over, and still he continued to hold her tightly against him, telling himself she was too breathless, too flown by champagne to be let go.

"Thank you, Miss Janet."

"Thank *you*, Lieutenant."

"My name is David."

"I know. My name is Jenny, David."

Her lips were upturned, parted, laughing.

Irresistible. He kissed them. Lightly, gently, persuasively.

Then, since she did not object, pull away, or withdraw her mouth, he kissed her again. He went right on kissing her, marveling, even as he tasted the sweetness of her mouth, at the wonderfully awakened response of her untried, unpracticed lips.

"Oh, my!" said Jenny when he finally gained the strength to let her go, and the apology now trembling on his lips died a-borning. He would not insult either himself or her with insincere words of regret for something that had filled the two of them with delight.

Still, he must be wise for them both. She was just—in her own words—half past fifteen, and with a tender knowledge of her he would have believed impossible one hour ago, he knew how desperately she yearned for someone to love.

He was trying to decide what to say when there was a sudden loud burst of music from below and the sound of mens' voices.

Jenny's face turned quite pale. He felt a quiver in the palms pressed against his chest. "I hear my father," she whispered. "The card game must be over."

"It's all right, Jenny," he soothed her gently. "You have been to the ladies' retiring room." Deliberately, he smoothed her hair back from her forehead with one hand and straightened the limp little garland of flowers at the back of her head. Then, smiling down into her eyes, he lightly ran the tips of his thumbnails across the curving line of her brows, a gesture so loving, so intimate, that even inexperienced Jenny knew it to be a caress.

A sob caught in her throat.

"You must smile now, Jenny," he told her steadily, "and descend the stairs. Hold your head high like a queen. Don't worry about the plate and glass; I'll take care of them. Never forget—you are light as thistledown and graceful as a fairy."

"I will never forget any of it, not ever."

"Then remember, in case we do not meet again this visit, that I will be back in another two years to claim my dance. The first waltz, Jenny, and your company for supper. Promise?"

"Oh, my, yes," breathed Jenny.

Seconds later, wrapped in the newfound self-possession of Miss Janet Rosellen, she inclined her head and started down the stairs. She knew he was watching her, though she never once looked back. She held her head high and proud, each step light as thistledown and graceful as a fairy.

Gibraltar
10th June, 1860

My dear Nell,

Obedient to your instructions, I subdued my natural modesty and sat to a Spanish artist who was recommended to me by Commander Colson's wife. The result is the miniature portrait to which this note is attached. I have it on the authority of no less a person than the artist himself that the finished work is only slightly flattering to the subject!

If you do not agree, toss away the picture but take care to retain the frame. It dates from the Moorish occupation and makes this wedding gift a little less an offering in egotism, since those minute rocks set in the gold scrollwork are jewels, not stones.

Nell dearest, I regret more than I can say that I will not be with you on your day of days. May you and Harry have a long and happy life together. If you are too modest, then tell him from me what a fortunate fellow he is to have secured you.

Always,
your devoted cousin,
David Fenton

*P.S. The enclosed envelope, as you may
see, is addressed to your young neighbor,
Miss Janet Rosellen. I would appreciate
your handing it to her privately. Do not
worry, Nell, she's a charming child, and I
will answer all your questions when I see
you.*

My dear Jenny,

*I am sending this letter under cover to
my cousin Eleanor, with full faith in
her tact and goodness of heart. She will
have made sure that it reached you without any public awkwardness or awareness.*

*I could not resist this last opportunity
to speak—if only with my pen—to you,
knowing Nell leaves Somerset so shortly
for her home in Hertfordshire with Sir
Harry Langley. Even were she not unable in the future to act as our interme-
diary, it will be long before I can write
again. I, too, will soon be unavailable, as
we expect to ship out again, probably for
the Indies, in less than a fortnight.*

*After so many months of idleness, I will
be glad to leave Gibraltar, grand and
awesome though the Rock may be, with
our signal flags waving proudly on its*

ramparts and our battleships guarding it below.

What troubles me is that our life here is all meaningless pomp and ceremony unrelated to the duties of a naval officer as I was taught and as I perceive them. More than half my life has been spent as a sailor. I entered the naval school at Dartmouth just before my thirteenth birthday (three years younger than your half past fifteen the night we met, my dear).

What ambitions I had! What dreams! With all the arrogance of youth, I expected one day to be the youngest admiral of the fleet—a most unlikely eventuality but one whose failure grieves me less than what has happened to our service.

Napoleon once said he would rather see the British on the heights of Montmartre than in possession of Malta. No doubt Gibraltar, too.

How our might has fallen! In our greed to acquire empire, we have destroyed rather than strengthened our navy. The present political strategy demands that we disperse our naval resources to every farflung corner of the world in search of enemies that do not exist. Nevertheless, to these corners our navy goes—our sol-

diers, too—and we sit wearying months and years.

Correction. In every corner of the Empire there is an embassy, thus an ambassador to give balls and a local potentate to tender receptions. Therefore, we do not just sit but are given to much bowing and scraping and, in our dress uniform, obligatory dancing. To say nothing of drinking.

I doubt that it has leaked back to our dear upright Island, Jenny, but in the Royal Navy more officers are court-martialed for drunkenness than for any other offense. And by drunkenness I do not mean the light-headed, stomach-churning, light-heartedness that a young lady sitting at the top of a flight of steps may achieve with a single glass of champagne.

Poor Nelson must be spinning in his grave.

I can see the little frown creasing your brow as you read my last paragraph, Jenny, sweet Jenny. You may erase it. I am not and will never be one of those officers. I have better uses for my money than to drain it away for Spanish wine and brandy. Indeed, my one extravagance is the purchase of pearls—special pearls as translucently pink as your *skin. If I exit the navy, it will be of my own will, on my own two feet (steadily). I shall only permit myself champagne dizziness when we two dance.*

How else could I look into your sea-colored eyes with pride as one day I intend to do?

Why do I know I need not apologize for this outburst, secure in my surety that you will understand all of it?

You must be sixteen by now, Jenny. By the time I come home again, you will be old enough in years (your heart is old enough already) to hear all the more important things I long to say to you.

> *Your friend and waltzing teacher,*
> *David F.*

To Mister and Missus Tom Ramsay in Fairburn Village

Dear Mum and Dad,

If our Maude is not to home to read this to you, I know you will find someone else, maybe Preecher. No need to worry, Mum, like you always do, it's all good news. Last month I was in a bit of trowbel under Captain Bullen—Captain Bully he

is and it's what we called him below
decks—and I got to admit things dint
look good for a whiles. Then all on a
sudden I was off the Vigilant and onto the
Consort under Captain David Fenton,
who I found out later had personally
rekwested me for his command.

It was a miracul, and you don't qwes-
tion miraculs. Commander Fenton is kin
to Lord Denby up at Carroll House but
that's not why he helped me. It's our Miss
Jenny. I would bet my six months grog
ration that he is sweet on her. Not that
he said so, mind, not to an ordinery seaman, but he did send for me after I transferred onto the Consort, and what he said
to me, frowning a bit, was that he ex-
peckted me to shape up and give no
trowbel.

I said yes sir, of course sir, and no sir.
Then he suddenly smiled and told me
that our Miss Jenny, God bless her (that's
me blessing her, not him) had asked him
to look out for me if he ever came across
me. It was the way he said her name that
made me suspeckt. Then he asked if I
ever wrote home, and when I said every
coupel months, our Miss Jenny had
learned us three, me and my sister and
brother to read and write, he wanted to
know would my mother have any objeck-

tions to giving Miss Jenny a letter from him.

I said no for you, Mum, meaning no objecktions, and yes you would. So this nice thik envelope inside mine has a letter for Miss Jenny from him, and he never said so but don't send it to the Abbey, Mum, but wait till Miss Jenny visits. His bleeding lordship Sir Loois probably don't think a sailor, not even an officer, is fit to court his daughter.

Dad I have the best model of the new ironclad to bring home to you. One of the colliers made it for me. The lad is a reel artist.

My love and respeckts to Maude and Johnny and you both.

From Your Son,
Eddy

My dear Jenny,

Eighteen months ago we met on the stairway of Carroll House. I remember our waltz. Your first. I remember our kiss. Also, I believe, your first? I remember how greatly honored I felt then—and still feel now—that I was the fortunate man chosen to share those two memorable firsts with you.

Will you take affront, Jenny, if I now add that what I remember most vividly and with the greatest joy about that night is the way we talked? We did so like two tried and true friends, friends of long standing, friends without barriers of restraint, friends with utter trust in each other.

I have never before or since felt so free to be myself as I did that wonderful evening, dear Jenny. I suspect—certainly, I hope—that you can echo the same sentiment.

Words are said to be cheap, but you made a request that night, and I answered it with a promise. I shall look out for Eddy Ramsay and be very good to him—for your sake—if he gets on my ship.

Well, I did at last come across Eddy Ramsay—after inquiring at any ship that came into port if he was on their list of seamen. Finally, the answer was yes.

He was in a spot of trouble at the time. Nothing serious, I assure you. Three bottles of brandy and a few pounds lost at cards provided a way out.

Ramsay is transferred to my ship, the Consort, and under my command now, as you may already know from his mother, who is in charge of getting this letter to you. I pray he may never be guilty of murder, mutiny, or mayhem, since, come what may, I must be good to him always for your sake.

Oh, Jenny, Jenny, though there have been changes and improvements that make me more optimistic about the future of the navy, if not my own future in it, still I cannot wait to get home. You are seventeen now, almost a woman. There was never such a lively, loveable girl as you, Miss Janet Rosellen, but the thought of the woman you will become . . .

Better not to think about it—not for a sailor thousands of miles away—

> Devotedly,
> David, your friend

Chapter One

THE THREE DAUGHTERS OF SIR LEWIS ROSEL-
len of Monksdale Abbey, situated five miles
outside the village of Fairburn in Somersetshire, were considered, after Lady Eleanor
Carroll's marriage had removed her from the
competition, to be the loveliest girls in the
neighborhood.

In the early winter of 1862, with England
still plunged deep into ostensible mourning
for the prince consort it had ever disliked,
London society was at a temporary standstill;
and Sir Lewis seized gladly at the excuse to
have his youngest daughter's coming out take
place economically at a local assembly nearly
a year before her eighteenth birthday.

His eldest daughter, Catherine, of course,
had been given the more elegant London
debut due her position as *the* Miss Rosellen.
Catherine, so darkly beautiful, so elegant, so
like himself, was deserving of the best. He

grudged her nothing, not even the awful expense of the court gown for her presentation at a drawing room.

When it came time for Catherine to dip low in a reverent curtsy and reach out her gloved hand to slip beneath the royal fingers she was about to kiss, Victoria had actually leaned forward and briefly touched her lips to Catherine's forehead. Seldom was the daughter of a baronet ever honored with that chaste salute reserved by the queen for the daughters of her dukes, marquesses, and earls.

It had been one of the proudest moments of Sir Lewis's life and yet strangely unsatisfactory in retrospect. Four years had gone by since that majestic moment, and, inconceivably, Catherine was yet unwed. She had received several offers, to be sure, but none that in any way matched the expectations of either father or daughter regarding to what the lady was entitled.

She must have wealth, that went without saying, but wealth below the rank of baronet was completely unacceptable to the pride of Catherine Rosellen.

Margaret, whose London debut followed Catherine's by two years, was not so nice in her notions. She considered wealth in any shape or form or lack of rank to be agreeable.

So Margaret danced every dance at her ball, dutifully attended the drawing room, and kissed the hand of the stout little matron with the ribbon of the Blue Garter across her chest —the queen did not honor the Rosellen family twice—and looked about her for a man of large fortune.

Her intellect, like her pride, being much less powerful than that of her elder sister, it came as a considerable shock to her to discover that men of large fortune seeking less well-dowered girls to marry were not nearly so numerous as the reverse case.

Somerset might suspect but was never informed that London had proved a sad disappointment to the elder Rosellen girls. Local opinion rallied behind them, and when Miss Janet made her debut and the fetes and breakfasts and balls and other mating rituals of the season continued, they came to be called the Three Roses.

Soon this name was broken down into more specific designations. Miss Rosellen, without great originality, was dubbed the Dark Rose. Her opposite, Miss Margaret, inevitably became the White Rose.

A little more imagination was bestowed on Miss Janet. Red Rose was the name she had expected herself, for it had never been denied by Jenny or any other that red was the true color of her hair. Other girls with tresses of similar hue could flatter themselves or be flattered by others into believing that their curls were coppery or auburn or perhaps even chestnut brown. Jenny was too painfully honest, too free of vanity to deceive herself or be deceived by others.

Had not her own father always called her hair—invariably prefacing the phrase with a contemptuous snort—Irish red? This phrase had, as such things do, circulated about the neighborhood, so that when it came time to give her a name, Jenny, without any of her father's disparagement in so describing her, was acclaimed the Irish Rose.

Her father considered the name quite good enough for her, but Jenny bore it with joyful pride. Had there not been a shining hour in her life when she had been told her hair was red and beautiful?

It had been more than two years now, but neither the mists of time nor one glass of champagne could dim the memory of warm lips pressed against hers, thumbnails stroking across her eyebrows like another kiss, the clasp of strong arms, and the dizzying delight of the waltz.

How many nights had she lain in bed, remembering all that had passed between them?

I cannot at the moment think of anything I would regret more than not meeting you tonight.

Never forget you are light as thistledown in my arms and graceful as a fairy queen.

You must smile now, Jenny. Hold your head high like a queen.

Prodigiously grown up she had become, seemingly overnight, whispered the servants, who all loved her. It was wonderful, the way she no longer turned pale or red or shrank back at Sir Lewis's barbs or the nasty remarks he was always directing at her. The Lord alone knew why, for a sweeter-tempered young lady it would be hard to find anywhere, always a "please" and a "thank you" and a pleasant smile, looking at a body as though she were a person, not part of the furnishings.

Other than the servants, no one was happier about the change in Jenny than her mother. Lady Caroline had grieved long and privately over Jenny's hurts, knowing any remonstration she made to Sir Lewis about his treatment of her favorite daughter would only encourage him to greater heights of sarcasm.

Suddenly there was a changed Jenny, a serene, confident Jenny, impervious to snubs and slights that before had set her trembling, smiling where once she would have winced. Poised in the drawing room, pouring tea in the parlor—and not a drop spilled—walking— Lord save us, there were times when little Jenny, the Irish Rose as they now called her, the servants agreed in awe, walked with her back straight and her head held up like she was the queen herself!

"You know, Jenny," Margaret said to her one day as they walked down the Abbey steps to where their horses and a groom were waiting, "your hair seems to be growing darker. It's not so Irish any more. I declare there are times when I think you look positively pretty."

Jenny's lips twitched. "Thank you, Margaret," she said gravely. "Coming from the White Rose, that is indeed a compliment."

As always, when confronted with one of life's absurdities, she wished that *he* could share it. Even with her darling Mama, Jenny thought fondly, it was not quite the same.

In the meantime, her darling Mama wondered and worried what was going on in Jenny's head. So often she would sit among a group of people, a faraway look in her eyes, a faint smile on her face for something far removed from the proceedings about them.

It was not a young man, Lady Caroline was sure of that. Jenny was frank and friendly with the young men of the neighborhood, but, her mother regretted, she kept them at a distance. Unlike Catherine, she was friendly; unlike Margaret, she was never flirtatious.

How could even Lady Caroline know that Jenny was waiting to keep a promise?

The first waltz, Jenny, and your company for supper.

Two years, he had said, and it was a little past that time. She did not even know where he was just now, whether he was in England or a far-distant country. Navy lists and newspapers were not always available to her.

If only Nell would come visiting, she could ask her, but Lady Eleanor was wintering in Hertfordshire, setting up her nursery.

Once during an afternoon call, she asked in a polite social way, "And have you had any recent news of your husband's nephew, Lieutenant Fenton, Lady Carroll?"

"There was a letter just last month," answered Lady Carroll comfortably. "Dear David is still on his ship, but as soon as it reaches port, I dare say he will come visit. He always does. Will you have tea or coffee, Jenny dear?"

"Tea, please, Lady Carroll," she answered quietly, helping herself to a small iced cake.

With Catherine's ears perked up and her mother's eyes on her, she did not dare venture more. She could have been direct with Lord William, but then he would have wondered.

She would just have to wait.

One day, the new Jenny knew, he would come to collect his waltz.

Chapter Two

In early spring of 1863, Lord William and Lady Carroll gave a dinner party for a distant family connection, Mrs. Congreve-White, who was visiting in Somersetshire with her married daughter, her son-in-law, and her nephew, Lawrence Nesbit, a handsome young man of twenty-four.

Mr. Nesbit had been orphaned young and reared by Mrs. Congreve-White. From his aunt he had received much spoiling and a very good opinion of his own worth. From his parents he had inherited silky blond hair, deep blue eyes, a high forehead, a delicate nose, a considerable fortune, and a paucity of intelligence.

He and Margaret Rosellen were destined by a happy fate for each other. They could sit and admire each other's looks, converse with the same joyful insipidness, and contemplate the many delightful ways to spend his money.

Sir Lewis having consented to the marriage with elated alacrity, the engagement notice was sped to the papers, the banns were read, and the wedding was set for early summer.

Those malicious people who suggested that the Rosellens were acting with indecent haste to ensure that such an eligible fish did not swim out of their net were generally held to be munching on very sour grapes indeed. At the privacy of one's own fireside, however, in most homes in the county, this uncharitable view was endorsed almost unanimously.

Summer came quickly, and with it the wedding. The White Rose was an angelically lovely bride in her gown of creamy silk trimmed with Alençon lace and worn with her Grandmother Rosellen's pearls. She was attended by her sisters, both dressed alike in gowns of pink tulle, which some said was an unfortunate color for poor Jenny and others—notably gentlemen—described as breathtaking with her Irish red hair.

The elaborate church ceremony was followed by a formal indoor luncheon at the Abbey and an outdoor frolic for servants and tenants. Then the ballroom doors were thrown open, and the guests flocked across the polished floors to where the musicians were tuning up.

Breathless after the first two dances, Jenny stood to one side of the ballroom, the pivot of attraction for three importunate young men, two cousins and a friend of her new brother-in-law, all of them clamoring for the first waltz.

Smilingly, Jenny uttered the practiced platitudes that passed for conversation on such occasions, wishing she could go off by herself. It had been a long, long day.

All at once her eyes blurred and the rose lace fan dropped from her suddenly shaking hands. Three dashing young men promptly stooped to retrieve it, and over their bowed heads Jenny stared out across the room, saying to herself, "I must stop this. I must not fancy that any man in naval uniform—or who holds his shoulders in just that way—."

Her gallants were still half-kneeling, her eyes had cleared, and the man in naval uniform, his shoulders held just so, was coming purposefully toward her.

"Oh, my!" said Jenny and took two steps forward out of the circle of her admirers.

She had dreamed of this moment hundreds of times, but the fulfillment exceeded all her hopes.

His face was more lean and browned, his body more vigorous, his eyes even darker and livelier. And his smile—how could any smile be so incredibly tender and inviting?

"It's the first waltz, Jenny."

"I've been waiting."

"I hope I didn't keep you waiting too long."

Even Jenny, so unlike other girls, could not quite bring herself to say, "I would have waited forever." She looked up at him, helplessly appealing, and her eyes said it all.

Something about the way he held out his hands and Jenny took them awed the three young men into silence. They stood by, unprotesting, one of them forlornly clutching a rose lace fan, as the sailor's arm went around Miss Janet and he whirled her onto the ballroom floor.

They waltzed without words for a few minutes. Then he spoke as he had in all her dreams.

"You are light as thistledown in my arms, Jenny, and you dance like a fairy queen. But you are not a plump little dumpling any more," he told her almost regretfully. "You are willowy as well as graceful."

"Oh, God!" groaned Miss Janet Rosellen in reply to this ardent declaration. "I think I am going to be sick."

One quick look showed him that the luminous pink skin was turning a pale green color, not unlike her eyes. There was a beading of sweat on her forehead, and she was breathing in short heaving gasps.

"Hold on one moment," said newly promoted Commander Fenton, and with naval alertness he had her off the floor and through a terrace window, where he was able to assist her stumbling footsteps down into the garden and lift her bodily behind a concealing bush.

"Go away!" wailed Jenny, leaning over the bush just in time.

Two hands attached themselves to her shoulders.

"G-g-g-go away," quavered Jenny again between heaves.

"Don't be silly!" said the crisp, assured voice of Commander Fenton. "Have you any idea how many midshipmen I have helped through bouts like this?"

Two more heaves, and it was over. He pressed a square of linen from his pocket into her hands and waited patiently while she wiped her mouth and patted her face dry.

"I'm not a m-mid-sh-shipman," Jenny stammered tearfully. "I-I wanted it to be so r-romantic for you."

At the thought of her recent foray into romance, she began to weep aloud, once again requiring the handkerchief she had just handed back to him so that she could dry her tears and wipe her nose.

He returned the limp piece of linen, unable any longer to restrain his laughter.

"I thought it was very romantic, Jenny," he assured her. "We did recognize each other instantly, and after only one meeting more than two years ago. We might easily not have known each other. People do change considerably. Look at you, a good stone lighter, and I, you may have noticed, have added a mustache." He fingered the silky light brown growth.

"Your eyes are the same."

"And yours—the same deep blue-green of the Mediterranean. If you knew how many times I saw them when I looked down at the water. And on night watches I would see your face in the North Star. I had some pearls strung into a necklace for you, Jenny. It is delicate and glowing and pink, just like your skin. Is that romantic enough for you?"

"Oh, my!" she gulped.

"What made you sick, Jenny?"

"Too much food, and I had three glasses of champagne," she admitted, mortified again, "on top of the excitement and the waltzing. You might as well know . . ." He understood even if she, in her innocence, did not, that it was the confession of complete commitment. "I always get sick—like that—when I become overexcited."

"I will try to keep the overexcitement in your life to a minimum," he promised with mock solemnity, "and since I doubt we will be able to afford much champagne or such rich food, that should take care of the problem."

"You truly don't mind?"

"I think it is far more romantic to hold your head while you are sick than to dance or flirt with or kiss any other girl in the world."

Jenny stared at him in sudden horror. It had never occurred to her that there might be other girls for him to kiss!

She bit her lower lip, wanting desperately to question him, knowing she did not have the right.

"We had better return to the ballroom," she said with artificial brightness. "I may be missed."

He had to take one running step to catch up, she started forward so quickly. He reached for her arm and tucked it into his, feeling the poker-stiffness of her body.

"Not since I kissed you, Jenny."

"I beg your pardon?"

"Except for some elderly hands, out of courtesy, both in the Indies and at Gibraltar, I have kissed no one since the night I kissed you." He grinned down at her. "Is not that what you wanted to know?"

Jenny turned as red as her hair. "Yes," she said baldly, her body suddenly alive and fluid again and pressing warmly against his.

At the door of the terrace, he paused briefly, bringing her to a halt, too.

"Can you say the same, Miss Janet Rosellen?"

Miss Janet Rosellen stared at him with haughty displeasure. "I do not kiss gentlemen I do not love," she told him loftily.

"Jenny, oh, Jenny!" With a supreme disregard for any wedding guests who might be going back and forth in such close proximity to the ballroom, he seized hold of her. Jenny rubbed the top of her head against his jacket, her heart singing, only now aware that for more than two years she had lived for this moment of being once more wrapped up in the wonderful warmth and well-being of arms hard and tight about her.

Reluctantly, he put her from him; reluctantly, she let him do so.

"When will you be eighteen, Jenny?"

"In six weeks."

"May I speak to your father then?"

"Not until you speak to me."

He sank down on one knee, one hand reaching out to her, the other pressed dramatically to his breast. "Miss Janet, it cannot be a secret to you that I have long esteemed and admired you. For some time now it has been my most fervent desire to engage you as my life's partner. I entreat—"

"Get up, you idiot!" cried Jenny, half laughing, half crying, and tugging at his hand. "Someone will see us."

"—and beseech you to be my wife," he finished buoyantly, bounding up and brushing the dirt of the terrace off his trousers.

"You idiot!" she repeated lovingly.

"Hardly a civil answer, dear girl, to an offer of marriage. Well, Jenny, will you have me?"

"Just you try to get away from me," warned the Irish Rose, her usual honest, completely inelegant self.

Chapter Three

IN LATER YEARS JENNY WAS TO REFLECT THAT six weeks was a very short period out of eighteen years to know perfect felicity and a happy confidence in the future.

Those six weeks were all she was destined to have.

She rode with David every day, at first with Lady Eleanor as chaperone—surely the most benevolent chaperone any pair of lovers could ask for. Nell developed a habit of dismounting halfway through the ride on the excuse of picking some flowers. She wandered so far in her search for unusual flora that they could count on her pleasant trick of disappearing each time for as much as a quarter of an hour.

These quarter-hours were given over to much pleasurable instruction that had not previously come Jenny's way. She learned first that to kiss did not just mean the pressure of two pairs of lips. There were incredible variations and in each one incredible delight.

High-necked gowns were burdensome—lesson two—while a low-cut dress was fashion's gift to men. A man's hand inside your bodice, in her own private opinion (provided the man was David), was God's particular gift to women.

As for crinolines—lesson three, also four, five, and six—they were the invention of the devil, with skirts and hoops and petticoats and ties and bows and all manner of cotton undergarments—damn it!—that not even a sailor used to dealing with tricky ropes and knots and rigging could contrive a solution for on a country road in the middle of summer.

It would be different, Jenny was informed, when they were married and there were no barriers of time or clothing between them.

"How different?" Jenny wanted to know, whenever David's profanity reached poetic peaks and the quivering of her own legs gave her a vague, faint, only half-recognized awareness that whatever it was he wanted, she wanted just as badly.

When she questioned him, however, Commander Fenton would remember somewhat ruefully that she was not yet eighteen and would make a rapid retreat.

"I'll tell you all about it when we are married."

"Now you sound stuffy, just like a husband," she told him once. "Why should *you* understand and I be kept in ignorance until I am married?"

"Damned if I know, Jenny," he admitted honestly.

"It's really not fair, you know," she said, plunking herself down under a tree and chewing reflectively on a stalk of grass.

"You're right, Jenny. The truth is—" He stood over her, looking down into the eager, open face. "I'm, well, embarrassed. I think it will be easier to show you than to tell you."

She nodded her head wisely. "I can understand that." Then her nose crinkled up and she dissolved in gales of laughter. "David, are you truly embarrassed?"

He nodded, red-faced.

Jenny laughed even harder. "B-but that's so r-ridiculous!" she gasped, wiping her eyes. "After your hands have been all over my b-bosoms, and th-those other things you did to them b-besides, and the way you k-kiss me with your lips w-wide apart."

"Jenny!"

"Well, you did."

He decided to carry this war into the enemy's camp and see if she still went on laughing. "I shall do a great deal more than that when we are married, Jenny."

"Oh, I know *that!* I wrote a letter to Margaret and she sent me a letter back, under cover to Nell, of course. She said the best part of being married is in bed. Will you show me immediately we go to bed, David?"

"We will retire right after the ceremony if you wish."

"Well, I wish, of course," said Jenny practically, "but there will probably be some sort of party first. Oh, David, I wish it were tomorrow. I want to be with you, and I want to *know*."

"I want to be with you, too, my dear love, more than I can say." He dropped down beside her under the tree, taking her hand in his. "As for knowing, let us, you and I, start a new trend in educating girls. As soon as they are old enough, you may tell our daughters."

"Daughters," said Jenny doubtfully.

"Daughters," he repeated firmly. "Three of them, I think, all with Irish-red hair."

Jenny rubbed her head against his jacket in her now familiar gesture of endearment, and he stroked the silken mass of her foxfire curls.

"You do realize, Jenny, that your father may insist on a long engagement? He will want to be more secure of your future."

"But you've just been made a commander!" cried Jenny, bouncing upright. "That's a wonderful promotion with so little influence as you have."

"That's just the problem, my love. It was a

piece of sheer luck, and in a peacetime navy, especially with so little influence, it's as far as I may go for many years. All I can offer you presently is a sailor's pay and a total fortune of three thousand pounds. I could not blame your father for demanding something more for you."

"I could!" said Jenny indignantly. "My dowry will be five or six thousand, I think. It's not a vast fortune, but between us we should have more than enough. And you *are* the Earl of Denby's nephew, which should count with Sir Lewis. It would look well in the notices to the newspapers. Besides which," she added, slanting that wise-old look in his direction, "I should think Papa might be as well pleased to have me out of the house. I *would* live with you, or in our own lodgings when you went to sea, would I not?" she asked in a sudden access of anxiety. "You would not leave me behind, would you, David?"

"You may even go to sea with me, if you have the heart for it, Jenny. You will never be left behind by any wish of mine."

Lady Eleanor went home to her husband the day after this exchange, and though meetings between Jenny and David were as frequent, they were never again quite so private.

Still, there were many snatched moments of happiness between them until her eighteenth birthday. During one such moment, turning aside into the rose garden at a picnic given by the Carrolls on the afternoon of the great event, he took the chamois-skin bag from inside his jacket and poured the string of pink pearls into her cupped palm.

"Oh!" cried Jenny rapturously. "They are so beautiful." She stroked the pearls reverently. "They're so pink, they glow at me."

"Like your skin, Jenny. Let me put them on for you. He stood behind her, fastening the clasp.

Jenny looked down at the pearls, luminous against her soft flesh.

"Oh, my!" she whispered, lifting them with her hands as he kissed her neck from behind.

"I have nothing for you," she mourned, turning around to him.

"Oh, yes, you do, Jenny," he whispered as she clung to him. "Indeed you do."

The next day Jenny brought her gold locket to him, a simple heart inscribed with the letter J in small diamonds. It had belonged to her Grandmother Conroy, that selfsame spirited English girl who had eloped with the objectionable Irish earl in the teeth of her family's opposition. "She was Janet, too. I was named after her," Jenny explained.

"I can't take a family ornament, Jenny," he protested.

"Then I can't keep the pearls," she retorted with an obstinate lift of her chin.

Yielding to this bit of blackmail, he fastened the fine thin chain about his neck and tucked the locket inside his shirt. "I shall wear it always for a keepsake and a safeguard," he vowed.

"And I your pearls," Jenny just had time to promise before Catherine shook off an unwelcome companion—the Carrolls' old governess —to join them.

As the three talked together of inconsequential matters, Jenny just touched her hand to the collar of her dress, signaling to him with that slight gesture and a glance of her bright eyes, that the pearls lay beneath her dress.

His answering smile showed his perfect comprehension even as he devoted the greater part of his conversation to Catherine for the scant few minutes she condescended to converse with him.

That Sunday after church services Commander Fenton sought a private interview with his prospective father-in-law. Sir Lewis was inclined to be more mellow than usual in midafternoon, his observant youngest daughter had prompted her lover previously. "He allows himself a double portion of Madeira after church and falls asleep in the library."

But even three glasses of Madeira had not mellowed Sir Lewis sufficiently. The honor of the relationship was declined with great vigor and not a little rudeness. He wondered—not to himself, but quite aloud—at the effrontery of the young man in making such an unreasonably ambitious application.

A daughter of Sir Lewis Rosellen—a family that had come over with the Conqueror—was not to be given, rather to be thrown away on an impecunious sailor who had only the trifling pay of his profession and a fortune of three thousand pounds to stand between the couple and a most degrading poverty.

"Three thousand pounds," echoed Sir Lewis, his handsome Rosellen features screwed up as though the idea of such a paltry sum was a bad smell in his nostrils.

"I would settle it all on your daughter, sir," said Captain Fenton, managing to maintain his composure and his temper, though the effort whitened his face and thinned his lips.

"Three thousand pounds," Sir Lewis repeated distastefully. "Young Nesbit settled fifteen on my daughter Margaret."

"It is true, as you have pointed out, that I am not rich, Sir Lewis," David urged doggedly, "but I do have a profession and the chance to rise in it. I am not without ambition. Just recently I consulted my uncle about participation in a business scheme in which he sees much merit."

"Business scheme!" huffed Sir Lewis. "I

hope my family is not so sunk in importance as to seek out alliances with business."

"My family is not without importance, too. On my father's side I am closely connected to the Carrolls."

"A distant connection, despite his kindness. There is nothing he can do for you. He has children of his own. No, no, you can expect nothing from him, and I wonder that he should not have prevented you from making an application that could only result in your discomfiture. Lord William has married his own daughter off very creditably, and he has too nice a notion of equality in marriage not to be aware that you, a mere sailor, are aiming much too high in expecting to rise through marriage to a Rosellen. A daughter of mine, I should hope, need not so despair of making an equal match as to take the first penniless sailor who offers for her."

"I love your daughter, and she loves me."

"My daughter is a fool, sir, but you, I fancy, would find it easy to love any young lady with her claims of birth and breeding, in short, a Rosellen."

"You are mistaken, Sir Lewis," came the clipped, cold voice of Commander Fenton. "The only impediment to my loving your daughter appears to be her surname. Am I to take it, then, that you will not even consent to an engagement, pending an improvement in the condition of my estate?"

"You are to take it, sir, that I categorically refuse to consider your offer. You say you are ambitious. Come to me when your ambitions have borne fruit. I would not give my daughter to you under any other condition."

Chapter Four

JENNY DID NOT HAVE TO WAIT TO HEAR FROM David about his unsuccessful suit. He was barely out of the house when she was bidden by a scared-looking housemaid to go down at once to the library where her father awaited her.

Sir Lewis had always been too indifferent to Jenny to play the heavy Victorian father in any other way than with verbal unkindness; but this time, as soon as the library door closed, shutting them in alone together, he thundered his disdain and disapprobation at her. To any listener it might have appeared that she had violated his ceaseless loving care and concern.

"I don't care whether he is rich," Jenny said at the end of a ten-minute tirade, unconsciously echoing David. "I love him, and he loves me."

"I have no patience with such folly. Do you

think," he asked crudely, "he would still love you if you were not the daughter of Sir Lewis Rosellen?"

"I know he would," retorted Jenny. "Probably more." And she promptly had her ears boxed.

"Go to your room, miss, and don't leave it again without my permission."

Lady Caroline visited her third daughter in her room that evening. Jenny was sitting in a rocking chair at the window, a basket on her lap. It had been smuggled up to her from the kitchen half an hour earlier, a table napkin discreetly covering the remains of a small broiled chicken, a wedge of cheese, an apple tart, and a juicy peach.

Jenny had disposed of most of the food and was concentrating on the peach.

Lady Caroline smiled faintly and decided to ignore this evidence of kitchen partisanship.

"Your father has been talking to me, Jenny. He will not consent to this marriage."

"Sir Lewis has already delivered his opinion," Jenny returned defiantly. "How can my father be so foolish as to believe that marriage to a Rosellen is the greatest honor that can befall any man? One would think our claims rated higher than the house of Hanover. For the love of heaven, Mama, Catherine has been out more than four years, and no royal prince has come a-courting yet!"

"Jenny," her mother told her carefully, "you must know that I do not quite share your father's regard for rank and consequence, so won't you please listen to me and believe that I am only concerned with what is best for you? I have nothing against Captain Fenton; in fact, I like him exceedingly. His profession does him no disservice in my eyes; I applaud it."

Jenny flung her peach pit into the basket. "Then why should we not marry?" she demanded fiercely. "He loves me. I know he does. Do you think, like my father, that I am so young and so silly as not to know when a man's feelings for me are sincere?"

"I think you are young, Jenny, but certainly not silly. The young man's feelings are obvious, which I have been noticing these last few weeks with great uneasiness."

"Why, Mama? Why should you be uneasy?"

"Love is not always enough, Jenny. One must live."

"I know Papa considers David's present circumstances pitiful, but surely with my dowry added to his income—"

"The problem is, Jenny," Lady Caroline broke in reluctantly, "that you do not have a dowry, except as your father wishes."

"I don't understand," said Jenny, more puzzled than concerned.

"Margaret, as you know, had her money

from your Grandmother Rosellen. Most of the Monksdale property and fortune is entailed on the heir. The sum set aside for you and Catherine jointly is almost ten thousand pounds, but how it is divided is entirely at your father's discretion."

"I understand." Jenny's lips twisted. "He could then, if he wished—and, oh, I am sure he so wishes—give it all to Catherine. My marriage to David would provide him with a good excuse."

"Jenny—"

"Mama, come now, do you think I don't know, that I haven't always known how he feels about me? As far as I can see, it provides another reason for me to marry David and leave this house once and for all."

Lady Caroline shook her head. "The desire to leave home is a bad reason to marry at just eighteen. You have no notion how struggle and privation can wear one down—what there might be for you to endure."

"I don't care," said Jenny proudly.

"And do you not care for David's interest either? Do you have any idea what a drain a young, untried wife would be for an ambitious naval officer? Is your love so selfish that you are willing to hold him back in his career?"

"You're only saying that to influence me against marrying David. You don't really care what happens to him!"

"I believe with all my heart," said Lady Caroline with a quiet sincerity there was no denying, "that a wife, a penniless wife, with no training to make her a helpmate to him, would at this juncture in his life drag him down; but you are justified in saying I am not greatly concerned with him, solely with you. Oh, Jenny, you are only eighteen! I, too, was eighteen when your father first came calling. He was handsome, ardent, vigorous, just like your David, seemingly the answer to any young girl's dream. He loved me. I, too, believed he would love me fervently and forever."

Rarely seen tears streamed down her face, melting Jenny's anger and resistance.

"My dear little daughter," her mother said tremulously, "I am not asking you to give your David up but just to wait one year. Surely one year is not too much to ask—a period in which to discover if your feelings can stand the test of time."

"A year can seem like an eternity," said Jenny slowly.

Lady Caroline laughed harshly. "A lifetime of marriage can be an even greater eternity. Oh, God, Jenny," the anguished entreaty seemed to burst from an overflowing heart, "do not let me know the pain of seeing you unable to go on loving, let alone respecting, the man you are forced to spend your life with!"

They stared at each other, white-faced, Lady Caroline's hands against her lips as though she would have taken back the awful admission she had just made, Jenny recognizing fully for the first time what her mother's life had been.

She took a step forward, and Lady Caroline moved toward the door.

"I should not have said that."

"It's nothing I didn't know, Mama. I just never realized—"

Lady Caroline turned to face Jenny again. Her face was pale but composed. "I had best join your father downstairs."

"Mama, tell Sir Lewis whatever you wish, whatever best serves our interests."

"What will the truth be, Jenny?"

Jenny hesitated, then said slowly, "I consider myself to be engaged to David, but it will remain unannounced. For your sake—not my father's—I will promise to wait one year to marry him. At the end of that year, nothing will stop me. Not lack of dowry, not considerations of fear, poverty, or privation. Is that acceptable to you?"

"Yes, Jenny."

"And I must be free to see David once more," she stipulated. "You may tell my father, if you wish, that I am administering his congé in person."

Those words of her own haunted Jenny later nearly as much as the memory of the six weeks of felicity. They proved to be prophetic, for David chose to take her acceptance of a year's delay as equivalent to handing him his congé.

"I want you to come away with me now, Jenny," he told her commandingly. "I have been making plans ever since I saw your father."

"You mean an elopement?"

"Yes. Why not? It isn't the way I would have chosen to take you, but I was up half the night looking at your grandmother's locket. *She* did it, Jenny, and you spoke proudly about her strength and spirit. You said she and your grandfather were happy all their lives."

"I promised my mother to wait one year. It's not so very long."

"Jenny, God knows where I will be a year from now. The admiralty is not concerned with the personal lives of its officers. It will not be so kind as to return me to you in exactly one year. When I ship out again, I will likely be gone for two or three years."

She cried out, and he repeated with a touch of ruthlessness, "Two or three years, Jenny, and I am not minded to wait them. Good God,

I have waited two already till you were old enough for me!"

"But I promised Mama," whispered Jenny, deathly pale.

"Who no doubt wishes to please your father. To please Sir Lewis Rosellen," he told her with angry arrogance, "forms no part of my plans."

Jenny pressed her hands against her temples, dizzied by a strange little flutter of pain.

"David, I don't think it's a very good idea for us to elope so that you can spite my father."

"You sounded very much like Sir Lewis Rosellen's daughter just then."

"And you don't sound at all like the David I fell in love with."

"If you are in love with me, then you will not hesitate to go away with me when I leave Somersetshire—no later than next week."

"Have I no choice, David?"

"I am leaving next week, Jenny—with you or without you."

"And if I am willing to come to you—as I am—will you not send for me in a year? Wherever you bid me come, to the outer Hebrides or the ends of the earth, I will gladly join you."

"Now or never, Jenny."

They were standing together again in Lady Carroll's rose garden, and the rich scent of her flowers perfumed the air. It was a long time before Jenny could smell roses without reliving the anguish of that parting.

"I love you, David, and I shall wait, praying every moment of the time that you will send for me in a year," she told him steadily.

She lingered a moment, but there was no change in his stony expression, no relenting in his rigid posture. There was no answer at all, which appeared to be all the answer she could expect.

Stepping lightly as thistledown, with her head held high like a queen, Miss Janet Rosellen walked away through the garden and out to her horse and the waiting groom.

Chapter Five

IN LATE SEPTEMBER, LADY CAROLINE WAS feeling poorly, and the apothecary and doctor at Fairburn both recommended the sea air at Brighton. After a family consultation, it was decided that Jenny should accompany Lady Caroline while Sir Lewis and Catherine visited London for the social season.

No one in Somersetshire conjectured aloud that Jenny was journeying to Brighton to forget her unfortunate love affair and that Catherine was traveling up to London for another attempt to procure herself a husband of baronet blood—at least not until the Rosellens were all safely on their way.

Unluckily, Jenny did not forget, and Catherine, having spurned a rich merchant and a poor knight, received no other offer. Sadly, Lady Caroline's health continued quite gradually to decline.

The original two months planned for their

stay in Brighton stretched out to two and twenty. Even though her health was not fully restored, Lady Caroline felt so much better for the sea breezes and the tangy salt air that on the advice of a local specialist who treated her, she prolonged her stay first one time, then another, eventually removing her daughter, her maid, and herself from cramped furnished lodgings to a cozy seaside cottage discovered by Jenny on one of her solitary rambles.

Jenny was as happy at Brighton as she could have been anywhere during this period of her life, certainly happier than under her father's roof.

If she had been able to believe that David would send for her when her year's waiting was over, the months would have sped by in enjoyment of her mother's company, free of her father's petty tyranny, busy and happy with tasks that were performed at Monksdale Abbey by a host of servants.

Remembering David's stony face when they had parted and his unrelenting silence ever since, Jenny nourished no false hopes that a summons would come. One hour on a stairway and six weeks two years afterward, she decided that first dreary winter, were to represent the sum total of her all too short love affair.

She was glad when summer came and then

the first anniversary of the day she had left him among the roses. The first year was over, proving her painfully right. "Now or never," he had said. Now or never, he quite obviously had meant.

She felt better to have it behind her and to know for sure that she must fashion some kind of life for herself as best she might.

Her first act of courage was to gather a bouquet of roses and to take them to the small conservatory-style room overlooking the sea, which they had made into a sitting room for her mother.

There Lady Caroline rested most afternoons; there she and Jenny greeted any callers who came to tea.

They were almost always joined by Sir Charles Melville, the specialist in nervous disorders who had removed to Brighton several years before to overcome depression after his wife died and because his own health could not withstand the rigors of a busy London practice.

He was a stocky man of medium height, with rugged, unhandsome features, weather-beaten from much beach walking, and only a shock of thick white hair to give him any air of distinction.

Sir Lewis would have deplored his looks as much as his careless dress and shabby boots. He would have deprecated Sir Charles's title as only a twelfth-generation baronet could depress such a new creation. Jenny had come to love Sir Charles with all her heart, at first for his compassionate care of Lady Caroline but later for the man himself.

Sometimes when the three of them sat together, eating sandwiches, cake, and tea, and chatting with cheerful ease, they seemed so like a family, a small happy family, that Jenny was often struck by the thought, "If only he had been my father!"

Later there were times, just looking at the two others, when she wondered if the same thought had not occurred to them. Even her own brief experience had made her wise in the exchanges of love, and there were looks that sometimes passed between the two, not less eloquent for being silent, and occasionally the lingering pressure of fingers as plates were handed over.

Jenny began to give them much more time alone together. She kept insisting that her mother invite Sir Charles to dinner not once or twice but three and four times in a week.

"Think of him rattling around alone in that great empty house," urged Jenny with pardonable exaggeration when Lady Caroline raised weak objections. "You know it makes a difference to us, too, Mama, to have a warm, witty, intelligent man at the dinner table."

Lady Caroline was diverted by a lover's desire to discuss the beloved object.

"He is all those things, isn't he?" she asked wistfully.

"He is all that one could want in a man."

"Yes," said Lady Caroline dreamily. Then, roused from her abstraction by an expression on her daughter's face she had come to know and dread, she added hesitantly, "Jenny?"

"No, Mama, don't let's talk about it," said Jenny in a hard, un-Jennylike voice. She added with pent-up fierceness, "Neither of us may have a happy ending like Grandmother Conroy, Mama, but why should you not at least enjoy Sir Charles's company while you may?"

From that day forward, Lady Caroline made no pretense about her feelings. Sir Charles came almost daily, either for dinner or to tea, and though he was no churchgoer himself, he sent his dilapidated carriage every Sunday to convey Jenny and Lady Caroline to services. Afterward he would join them for the entire afternoon.

Sir Lewis Rosellen, at every change of season when travel was practicable and with all the pomp that could be lent by servants, excess luggage, and ceremony to a journey by rail and carriage, descended on his wife and daughter for a rigidly formal, mercifully short ritual visit. Catherine came with him only once.

On such occasions, with no word or hint needing to be given, Sir Charles almost disappeared from their lives, paying only the official weekly call to examine his patient and consult with her husband.

They had occupied the cottage for only six months when, on the first night of one of his visits, looking disdainfully about the modest interior of the bright little cottage, Sir Lewis avowed his intention of restoring his family to its own proper home.

Jenny cast a look of bleak despair at her mother; Lady Caroline gave a warning shake of her head and a brief reassuring smile.

The next day, Sir Charles was summoned to the Rosellens' cottage, and they sat awaiting him while the twelfth baronet cast his usual aspersions on the first.

"*Sir* Charles Melville—made baronet for doctoring—I must say the queen is overly lavish in heaping her honors on men whose fathers would not have been allowed through the front door of *my* father's house. The fellow sends in his bills with promptitude, I don't doubt, hey?" he said to Jenny, who managed such matters for her mother now.

"Doctors must eat, too, Papa," she said, not pertly but in the manner of one imparting information.

"I dare say he does well enough since it is known hereabouts that he is consulted by Lady Caroline Rosellen."

"He is an excellent physician and most properly grateful for our recommendation," said Lady Caroline soothingly, with another warning look at Jenny.

After a visit of not more than five minutes closeted with Lady Caroline, her maid in attendance for the benefit of Sir Lewis, the two men spoke together for twenty minutes behind closed doors.

When Sir Charles had left the house, Jenny was summoned to Sir Lewis in the parlor. She found him walking about the room, pale and distraught. He spoke to her more naturally than he had in years.

"Jenny, I had thought to have you and your mother return to Monksdale with me, but Sir Charles informs me I must on no account take your mother from Brighton. To do so would be to shorten her life."

"Sir Charles really stirred him up," thought Jenny admiringly.

"She will need you with her, of course," Sir Lewis continued.

"Of course, Papa," said Jenny demurely.

"The later progress of her illness will require much personal care and attention."

Jenny's mouth went dry and her hands became clammy; her heart began a wild, frightened pounding. Sir Charles might be canny, but he was not cruel. He might toy with the truth a little in a good cause, but he would never be so unethical as to tell a man that his wife was—was—

"Is Mama dying?"

"Sir Charles says—he is quite agreeable to my calling in another specialist—he thinks with proper nursing that perhaps she may have another year or two. Sit down, Jenny. Drink this." He thrust her into a chair with a rough kind of kindness she had never known from him before and held a glass of wine to her lips. "I am sorry," he said distractedly. "I thought perhaps you were previously aware, that Sir Charles might have said something to you."

"I knew Mama was not getting better," Jenny faltered, "but I did not think—what ails her?"

"Some disorder of the nervous system. Sir Charles appears to have written several books on that very subject. Jenny, are you in control of yourself now? If so, I think I had best go to your mother."

"Yes, please do," said Jenny, twisting a handkerchief round and round in her hands. "I need to be by myself for a bit to—to—I am fine."

Much later that afternoon she had a second interview with Sir Lewis.

"Your mother shows remarkable courage and fortitude," he told Jenny, a note of admiration that had not been there for many years creeping into his voice. "She is fully cognizant of her situation—has been for some time—and her concern is all for us. She knows my chief duty must be to Monksdale and is content to have Catherine take her place in the present as she will eventually do in the future. Your attendance, of course, I have assured her."

He paused, changing the plain statement into a question.

"Of course," confirmed Jenny. "Nothing—no one—could make me leave her while she needs me."

So perhaps it was as well, said her desolate heart, that the summons from abroad had never come.

Chapter Six

LADY CAROLINE WAS ASLEEP ON THE LOUNGE in her conservatory room, where she now spent all of her days. Jenny sat close beside her, balancing a teak lap desk on her knees and busily transcribing the last batch of notes she had received from Sir Charles.

During the past five months she had acted as his amanuensis, greatly hastening the progress of his new book, *Diseases of the Muscular System.*

She paused for a moment to rub her aching wrists and saw that Lady Caroline's eyes were open and staring at her in rather melancholy fashion. She jumped up to put the desk and papers on top of a small serving table, then returned to the bed.

"Mama, are you in pain? Shall I get your drops?"

"I feel fine, Jenny. I need nothing."

"Then why do you look at me so?"

"I need nothing except your forgiveness, Jenny."

"How nonsensical! You have done nothing that needs my forgiveness." Jenny knelt by the bed. "I love you, Mama."

Lady Caroline's frail hand stroked her daughter's Irish-red hair.

"I should not have made you promise, Jenny. It was your life, your choice to make, but I thought to spare you suffering."

"Shall I tell you something, Mama?"

It was a rhetorical question, which she answered herself before Lady Caroline could reply.

"I would have broken the promise. In fact, I tried to—the very next day. I hardly slept at all the night after David and I quarreled, and when I arose early in the morning I knew that nothing mattered, not pride or promises or even you, Mama, only the feeling between David and me. So I went down to the stables before half past seven, and Jimmy saddled my horse for me and agreed to tell no one that I had gone out. I rode over Farmer Elton's back fields to the Carrolls', and when I got to their stables they told me he was already gone. He had left by Lord William's coach just a little past dawn."

She rocked back on her heels. "His stubborn pride had not permitted him to wait and see if I would change my mind or even to attempt one more time to change it for me. The wound to his self-esteem from Sir Lewis proved greater than his love for me. It still does, or perhaps there is simply no love left. In either case, you must stop blaming yourself, Mama. A little loving patience, and I would not have been able to resist anything he asked of me. So it is David, not you, I sometimes find it hard to forgive."

There was a long, thoughtful silence before Lady Caroline said gently, "Don't let your pride stand in the way of your happiness, Jenny."

Jenny rose from the floor. "The next time I fall in love," she said gaily, "I shall exhibit no pride at all. I think I heard a carriage. Sir Charles must be here."

"Did I hear my name?" asked a gruff voice at the door, and Sir Charles entered the conservatory, darting a quick, keen glance at the pale face against the lounge pillows.

"Charles," she said glowingly, holding out both hands.

Jenny had lately seen with gladness, not with envy, that when he was with her, her mother had eyes for no one else. Quietly she passed out of the room, closing the door behind her.

Her mother's maid appeared with the huge tea tray, and Jenny shook her head. "Not just yet, Peggy. Lady Caroline will ring when she wants her tea."

With a smile of conspiracy and understanding, Peggy returned to the kitchen with Jenny trailing in her wake. Nothing in life would have horrified Sir Lewis Rosellen more than the sight of his daughter seated at a kitchen table with the cook and his wife's maid, the three drinking their tea and chatting companionably together, waiting for Lady Caroline to ring the bell.

A month before Jenny's twentieth birthday, Sir Lewis paid his usual spring visit to Brighton and was pleased to find his wife in good spirits and her physical condition apparently no worse than the previous autumn.

About a month after Jenny's birthday, there came an afternoon when Lady Caroline was too weary to sit at the luncheon table.

"I am not really hungry," she replied tiredly to the suggestion of a tray.

"Do you want to go to the conservatory, Mama?"

"I think perhaps I would rather go to my bed."

Sir Charles led her on his arm out of the room and supported her up the cottage stairs. Jenny and her maid undressed her and put her between the sheets. She fell asleep almost immediately, and Jenny left her with Peggy and returned to the dining parlor.

Sir Charles sat at the head of the table, his food untasted before him, his head lowered into his hands. He lifted a face ravaged with grief to Lady Caroline's daughter.

"Jenny, I think you had better send for your father," he suggested hoarsely.

"How long?"

"Days. Weeks. Perhaps a month."

"Then why cannot she be left in peace with you and me?" Jenny cried.

"My own feelings are too much involved for me to make such a decision. I want to do what is right, but—"

"I will make the decision then!" Jenny interrupted impetuously. "What is right for her is peace of mind. She needs contentment, and she can only have that if you are always by."

"Thank you, Jenny."

"Dear Sir Charles." She bent a moment to touch her tear-drenched cheek to his. "You have been more my father in this short time than ever Sir Lewis was, and what you have given m-my m-mother—"

She burst into tears and ran from the room.

The next day Lady Caroline's bed was brought down to the conservatory, and it became her sick room. She never left it again. Sir Charles moved into the cottage to be constantly by her, and he and Peggy and Jenny divided her nursing.

On the day five weeks later when he said,

"A matter of hours, child," Jenny arranged for a telegraph message to be sent to her father.

"I shall leave you with Sir Charles while I have lunch," she told her mother cheerily. She kissed Lady Caroline's wasted face, smiled, and left them alone together.

When Sir Charles came out to the garden where she had sat motionless for almost three hours, she understood that her mother was dead.

Jenny knew that Lady Caroline would have preferred to be buried in the little cemetery overlooking the sea, a half-mile from Sir Charles's great shabby house.

But it was not to be.

The arrangements made by Sir Lewis were all that were proper and honorable and befitting the twelfth baronet's wife and the daughter of even an Irish earl.

The body was brought back to Monksdale and properly interred just beyond the great mausoleum that held the baronets of two centuries and countless Rosellen relics and children. Lady Caroline lay next to her three-week-old son.

"It doesn't matter, child," Sir Charles had tried to comfort her. "It's just a body from which the spirit has flown. Your true mother is with us always."

"I know," Jenny had agreed even as she cried and clung to him. "But I can't bear to leave Brighton—to go back to Monksdale without her."

"Jenny, I promised your mother I would take care of you, and I mean to do so. It will be my joy. You must go home for the funeral and do all that is proper . . . but in less than a year you will be twenty-one and not subject to your father's authority. If you want to come back to Brighton then, I will keep the cottage for you. Perhaps Peggy can stay and take charge of it."

Peggy stayed gladly. No more than Jenny did she wish to return to Monksdale without Lady Caroline.

The knowledge that the dear little cottage at Brighton was waiting for her was Jenny's only comfort in the dreary weeks that followed.

After the funeral and mourning visits were over, life settled down to what it had always been at Monksdale; Jenny had forgotten in nearly two happy years of release how formal, how artificial, how dull life at Monksdale could be.

She had forgotten the excruciating boredom of drawn-out family dinners, the inanity of the trivia that constituted conversation between her father and her sister.

She found herself bursting with a resentment she acknowledged to be unjustified at the easy way Catherine presided in her mother's place, as though Lady Caroline had never been.

Henry Rosellen, her father's heir, had come from Derbyshire for the funeral. He was a tall man in his forties, with those very Rosellen features that appeared in family portraits for generations, but not the Rosellen superciliousness or pride.

Catherine had previously met him on her London visits, and it had always been Jenny's secret suspicion that she was interested in the man, not so much for himself as because he was her father's heir. The difference in age, even in breeding and education—for Henry Rosellen had been educated poorly by an impecunious widowed mother—meant nothing to her compared to the fact that one day he would be Sir Henry Rosellen.

Why no engagement had resulted, Jenny could not determine. If Catherine had been willing, then it must be Henry who had held back. Perhaps, based on his expectations, he was aiming higher in terms of fortune. If so, he had apparently experienced a change in feelings, for he was certainly making every attempt to please and court Catherine now.

The solution was given to Jenny all too shortly when Sir Lewis summoned her for a private meeting in the library.

Blustering because there was some embarrassment in the telling, he informed Jenny that her sister's engagement to Henry Rosellen would be announced when the strict period of their mourning was over.

"I am very glad for Catherine," said Jenny sincerely, though the walls of Monksdale seemed to be enclosing her in an even more stifling grip. Miss Rosellen was difficult enough to live with; the future Lady Rosellen would be intolerable!

Sir Lewis coughed. "Catherine's dowry is set at ten thousand pounds." He fiddled with some ornaments on his desk. "Henry is not a rich man, and his position—his future position demands that he—in short—"

"In short," said Jenny crudely, "he will not take her with less. May I ask what is left for me?"

"With the little I may be able to add," he coughed again, "twelve hundred pounds."

"I see," said Jenny with a bitter little smile. "Tell me, Papa, if your heir won't take Catherine with less than ten, who do you suppose will offer for me with my twelve hundred?"

"As long as I live," said her father, affronted, "you will never lack for a good home."

"But you are unlikely, in the course of nature, to live as long as I do," Jenny pointed out matter-of-factly. "What do I do then?"

"Henry has assured me—and did I not hear

Margaret begging you to come home with her when she attended your mother's funeral?"

"So I am to be a dependent on one or both of my sisters, something between a governess and a maid, unpaid, of course, glad for my food and lodging, my money to serve as a dress allowance."

With genuine curiosity she asked him, "Tell me, sir, why did you not let me marry David? He had a profession and three thousand pounds. Why should he have been considered unfit to marry a girl who had twelve hundred and no future? I am the daughter of a baronet —so—he was the nephew of an earl."

Her father muttered something about changed circumstances—blood—the inability to foresee the future—

He was making his excuses more to himself than to her, for Jenny did not stay to hear them but fled upstairs to her room.

Chapter Seven

IT WAS A QUIET SUMMER AND AUTUMN FOR THE Rosellens, who could not, during their period of mourning, share in the usual social activities of Fairburn.

Jenny rose every day and took long walks. She spent hours reading and writing to Sir Charles in the garden that had been Lady Caroline's delight.

Her body sat in the drawing room every evening while her mind was far away, dreaming of Brighton.

She was seriously considering Margaret's reiterated demands for a visit as a way to relieve her boredom—the new baby was bound to be an object of greater interest than anything Monksdale had to offer—when she heard that Lady Eleanor was coming to Carroll House the following week.

She decided instantly to delay her visit to Margaret until Lady Eleanor's was over.

"How wonderful to see Nell again!" she told herself, knowing full well she was acknowledging only half the truth. Nell would have news of *him*.

In bed that night, slow tears trickled down her face. Complete, unrelenting silence for more than two years now. What kind of fool was she to think that news of him would make any difference?

Still, she went to pay her call at the Carrolls' in a flutter of spirits she had not known since Commander Fenton had gone away.

She had hoped it would be a quiet visit, just the family and herself, with perhaps the opportunity to go off quietly with Nell for a few minutes.

Instead, it appeared from the sound of voices that greeted her as the butler led her toward the drawing room that half the county had chosen that morning to call.

Stifling her dismay behind a company smile, Jenny greeted Lady Carroll and then found herself being warmly welcomed and kissed by Nell.

They had no sooner finished with cries of how good it was to see each other when Lady Eleanor's forehead wrinkled up, and she said in a hurried undertone, "Jenny, I must warn you—tell you—"

Her warning was never completed, for the sound of new arrivals was heard, the door was once again thrown open, and Jenny, standing half-paralyzed, knew what Nell had been about to say.

There was no difference in his appearance, except in his dress. He wore breeches, boots, and a blue riding jacket. He was as vital, as vigorous, as sun-browned, and his eyes were as vividly dark. His light brown hair persisted in curling over the ears as it had always done, and he still sported the slight, silky mustache.

There was a young lady clinging to each of his arms, two very pretty young ladies indeed. After a minute of doubt, Jenny's mind clicked in recognition. The Hargrave sisters, Doris and Celia, daughters of the squire; the eldest brother had been one of Catherine's suitors five years before.

They had not been out when Jenny went to Brighton, and here they were all grown up. Doris—or was it Celia?—looked adoringly at the back of his head; Celia—or perhaps Doris—fluttered her eyelashes at him in flagrant flirtation.

"How long has he been here?" Jenny asked Nell quietly.

About to lie, Nell met Jenny's unflinching look and told her honestly, "Six days, Jenny."

Six days. Not a word. Not a sign. Not even a note about her mother. Six days, when it would have taken only six minutes.

Now or never, Jenny.

What a simpleton I have been, deluding myself, Jenny thought dispassionately. In spite of her fine assurances to Lady Caroline, all along she must have nourished secret hope. Some day he would come back to England. Some day he would come back to her.

Lady Carroll had detached her nephew from Celia and Doris Hargrave and was moving about the room with him, performing introductions where they were needed. He was smiling and bowing with practiced ease, shaking hands, till he got to Jenny.

"How do you do, Miss Rosellen?" he said in a cool, crisp voice, with the most distant of bows.

"How do you do, Captain Fenton?"

Lady Eleanor had slipped her arm through Lady Carroll's and somehow managed to whisk her away. David and Jenny were alone in a sea of people.

"Just plain Mister. I resigned from the navy more than two years ago, having come to agree with—certain others—who did not see much future in it for me."

Jenny's cheeks reddened with anger and hurt, knowing this thrust was meant for her. He saw the surge of color in her pale face and relented a little.

"I am—I was sorry to hear about your mother. I know you must miss her greatly."

"More than I can say," said Jenny softly.

"Janet, dear, how good to see you out and about again," proclaimed the booming voice of Miss Pectin, the vicar's sister, who kept house for him.

While Jenny returned this greeting, Doris Hargrave—or perhaps her sister Celia—claimed David's attention, and when Jenny was able to turn back to him, the two of them were already taking a turn about the room.

She looked about for Nell, counting the minutes until this nightmare call could be ended, but her cup of bitterness was not yet full.

Some of the ladies consented to entertain, and several rows of chairs were set out while the first performer sat down to the piano. Jenny, who had been about to slip out of the room and out of the house, found herself forced by politeness to accept a seat offered her in the second row. An unhappy mischance placed her just behind the all too recognizable shoulders of David Fenton and next to him his cousin Nell.

The young lady at the piano fussed first with her music and then with her seat, and during that two-minute wait, Jenny heard Lady Eleanor whisper quite audibly to David, "Did you see Jenny?"

"I saw someone who resembled the Jenny I used to know. She looks hideously thin and haggard."

"She is in mourning. She has been through a great deal," came the low, indignant reply. "Anyhow, that wasn't what I meant, David. Naturally, I know you *saw* her. What I meant—"

"I know what you meant. My dear cousin," he drawled in a horridly patronizing way, "you are being foolishly romantic. That boy-and-girl affair of ours is long since over. Hush now—Miss Bentley is about to play."

Rude or not, as Miss Bentley began what was fortunately a noisy concerto, Jenny rose from her chair and tiptoed from the room.

She packed her trunks that very afternoon, and in the evening she informed her father and sister that she planned to leave for Margaret's home the next day.

Catherine made no attempt to hide her satisfaction, and Sir Lewis, actuated by strong feelings of unaccustomed guilt, was most assiduous in making arrangements for her journey. He even handed her a much more generous allowance for her stay than was usual with him.

The sum he gave her, together with all the remaining cash money of Lady Caroline's from their cottage expenses (which Jenny had prudently withheld from her father) furnished her with more than enough for her needs.

As soon as the coachman was out of sight of

Monksdale Abbey, Jenny gave him a change of orders. She had no intention now of going to Margaret's, and the coach headed instead for the nearest railway town.

She was forced to wait more than two hours at the station. After writing out a wireless telegraph to be sent to Sir Charles, she spent most of that time sitting on one of her trunks, dwelling ceaselessly on words she would have given her twelve-hundred-pound dowry to have forever erased from her memory.

Hideously thin and haggard. . . . Boy-and-girl affair is long since over. . . .

It was a long and tiring journey, less comfortable even than usual, for—looking to the future when not a single penny must be spent thoughtlessly—she had bought a second-class ticket.

There was no sign of Sir Charles's ancient carriage when she stepped down from the railway car and looked hopefully about, so her last necessary extravagance was to hire a chaise to drive her to the cottage.

She debated going to Sir Charles's first and then decided against it. Perhaps the telegraph had gone astray, or he might be away on a visit.

Night was setting in, and she would do better to get herself settled at the cottage, which Peggy would have kept in order. The thought of Peggy's warm welcome and the hot cup of tea she would bring to her bed . . . and perhaps after she had rested and refreshed herself, Peggy would brush out her hair; she had such a magic hand with a brush. Her head—Jenny rubbed it—was beginning to ache abominably. The railway carriage had been stiflingly close, and the chaise had a musty odor. It was beginning to rain a little, but she did not care. She put down the window and thrust out her face, with a gasp of relief for the fresh sea air, breathing in great lungs full.

"Just round the bend here and take the right fork," she directed the coachman, and minutes later she leaned forward eagerly, peering through the dusk for her first glimpse of the cottage.

For a moment she thought she was losing her mind. There were the two great oaks, leaning toward each other like lovers, and just behind them should stand the cottage; but instead there was nothing, just a great empty space.

"Stop! It's right here."

"Ain't no house here, mum."

Jenny threw open the door and jumped down the instant he brought the horses to a halt, twisting one ankle slightly. She held onto the coach door, gritting her teeth against the pain. As it subsided, she hurried along the gravel path, the coachman right behind her.

The cottage lay on the ground about her, reduced to a blackened heap, odd timbers jutting upward between the foundation stones.

"There's been a fire here, Miss," said the coachman, not without sympathy. He looked up at the darkening sky. "It's coming on to rain heavy. Best you get back inside the coach."

"Yes," said Jenny in a faraway voice, "best I do."

"Where to now, Miss?"

"Sir Charles Melville's, off the main Brighton Road." She forestalled his next question. "I'll direct you."

When he turned into the broad driveway that led to Sir Charles's sprawling seaside house, Jenny unconsciously braced herself; but the house stood there, big and blessedly lighted.

Painfully aware of her swelling ankle, Jenny let out her breath and accepted the coachman's help in descending.

"Please bring the trunks."

She grasped the wrought-iron railing and pulled herself up the wooden steps, barely conscious of the wind whipping her skirts and the rain drenching her.

She banged the door knocker several times, and when there was no immediate response she leaned against the door, pounding it with both hands, aware in some vague recess of a mind that seemed not quite to belong to her that her control was slipping.

"Sir Charles. Please, Sir Charles," she sobbed aloud.

The door was flung open so suddenly that she staggered across the threshold and almost fell to her knees in the hallway.

An arm kept her upright, an arm that belonged to someone who echoed her cry for Sir Charles.

The next moment his arms were around her. The dear, weatherbeaten face crowned by the shock of white hair was peering anxiously into hers.

"Jenny, my dear Jenny, what on earth brings you here at such an hour and in such a state?"

He was untying the bows of her bonnet as he spoke, unbuttoning her short light cloak.

"Only a mantelet on such a damp night. Why, you are soaked through to your skin, child. You must get out of these wet garments immediately. James, bring Peggy here to me."

With great effort Jenny lifted a head that seemed much too large and heavy to be supported by her neck. "Peggy," she whispered. "She is here? I went to the cottage."

"Oh, my dear child. I had planned to write

you of the fire after a time. I thought to spare you till you were more able to bear it. Jenny, what brings you here like this?"

"Don't *you* want me either?" wheezed her husky, breathless voice.

"Dear child, I have missed you more than I can say. I am just concerned for—"

Miss Janet Rosellen had no strength left to keep her standing while she listened to his concern.

"Then that's all right," she said in a sighing whisper. She put out her hands and, before he could grasp them, performed the most properly Victorian and un-Jennylike act of her life, crumpling at his feet in a dead faint.

Chapter Eight

JENNY OPENED HER EYES TO BRIGHTON sunshine and the marvelous fishy fragrance of the sea drifting in through an open window, slightly swaying the cream lace curtain. She lay in the middle of a big four-poster bed, which had been stripped of its heavy hangings. It was a large, cheerful chamber papered in a design of cool green ferns and sprightly daffodils. A pair of upholstered chairs and several pieces of unfashionable white-painted furniture were scattered about.

It was a comfortable room, a pleasing one, Jenny decided, and she wondered in a detached way how long she had lain in it.

"Oh, you're awake, Miss Jenny."

"Peggy, I'm so glad to see you."

"And me to see you, too, Miss Jenny. Now don't cry," she added hastily. "Sir Charles doesn't want you upset." She sniffed herself, used a corner of her apron to blow her nose, and rushed out of the room, bellowing for Sir Charles.

He was beside the bed in a moment and, after touching Jenny's forehead and counting her pulse, nodded with great satisfaction.

"How long have I been here?"

"You arrived the night before last. Your telegraph came the next morning." He pulled one of the bentwood chairs over close to the bed and sat down in it, retaining her hand. "You were in a high fever through the first night and most of yesterday; but you have a strong constitution, my dear Jenny, and no thanks to your imprudence," he shook his head at her in smiling reproach, "you seem to have rallied remarkably well."

He pressed her hand. "Do you want to tell me about it, Jenny? If you would rather not—"

"It was panic, I expect, and perhaps delayed shock over Mama," said Jenny overbrightly. "I never realized before that I was the hysterical type of person." She tried to sit up, shuddering a little. "I just suddenly felt as though the world was falling in ruins all around me, and there was no one to run to but you."

As briefly as possible, she told him about Monksdale and Catherine's engagement to Henry Rosellen, her dowry, and the devastating meeting with David.

"There was only you, Sir Charles," she said again.

"I am more honored than I can say that you turned to me."

Jenny blinked rapidly a few times, determined not to cry. "I can't go home again; I won't," she said. "All the day's journey to Brighton, I tried to plan. I don't want to put dear Mrs. Breedon out of a situation, so I can't ask you to take me on as your housekeeper. But I could be a housemaid part of the time— Peggy and I did the dusting and polishing and made beds together at the cottage—and if you are still working on your book you might use me as your amanuensis again, and I can arrange the flowers and help you with your correspondence, perhaps make out the menus. Dear Sir Charles, please let me stay. I have a little money for my immediate expenses. I know you have not much yourself, but I won't be a burden, I promise you. All I want is a room and my food."

"A burden," he repeated incredulously. "Jenny, whatever gave you the notion that I am poor?"

She stared at him blankly for several seconds. "Why, your clothes, I expect," she said slowly, glancing at him apologetically. "They always seemed so shabby, and your carriage so run-down. The house as well. I know it's large, but it always looked shabby, too, and the grounds not kept up. Besides, I knew you gave up the rest of your practice after Mama became so ill." She cleared her throat nervously. "You mean you are *not* poor?" Jenny asked him bluntly.

His eyes twinkled. "Quite the opposite."

"Oh," said Jenny. Then, rather helplessly, "Oh," again. Her fingers played nervously with the coverlet. "Then I suppose—"

"You mean you are willing to ask help from a poor friend but not a rich one?" he asked gently. "I never thought you were a snob, Jenny."

"Oh!" she said again indignantly. Then, "You're laughing at me, Sir Charles. I suppose I deserve it."

"You do, indeed. I must confess that clothes and carriages and houses have no interest for me except in the strictest sense of their utilitarian purpose." He grinned broadly. "Being wealthy, I can afford to be eccentric, unlike the middle class on the rise, who must care what other people think."

"Well, then, Sir Charles, dear *wealthy* Sir Charles," said Jenny, with the first genuine smile that had appeared on her face in months, "may I stay and work for you, with perhaps a small salary added to the food and lodging?"

Sir Charles, to her surprise, did not return

her smile but leaned back in his chair, speaking very seriously.

"You may, if that is what you still wish," he said, "after hearing my alternative proposal."

All at once he seemed a bit awkward and unsure of himself. "This plan, I must tell you, was originally suggested to me by Lady Caroline during one of the many times we discussed how best I might secure your future."

He added hesitantly, "It is no secret to you that I loved her and I came to regard her beloved daughter as mine." Then there was a long pause.

"I am waiting to hear your proposal, Sir Charles," Jenny said at last.

"Proposal is the correct word, Jenny. Strangely as it may strike you, Car—Lady Caroline first suggested that I might best take care of you as a daughter if I were to make you my wife."

Jenny sat bolt upright. "Sir Charles!"

"Absurdly enough, considering the thirty-year difference in our ages, it would destroy your reputation if you, a single woman, stayed on here with me."

"As though I would care about the opinion of anyone who had such thoughts of either you or me!" said Jenny scornfully.

"I must care for you then," Sir Charles told her firmly. "I cannot keep my promise to your mother by destroying your good name. Rightly or wrongly," he reminded her, "in our society marriage is still a woman's greatest safeguard. I am offering you the protection of my name, my wealth, my presence, nothing more. You would be Lady Melville to all the world, but only you and I would know that Lady Caroline was the love of my life and Lady Melville was my daughter."

"I can't accept the sacrifice of your life," Jenny protested. "A man in his fifties is still—you might meet someone else one day, Sir Charles."

He smiled and shook his head, and even in her own ears her voice did not sound too convincing. No more than he did Jenny believe that the man who had been privileged to receive her mother's love—

"It is you who will fall in love again one day, Jenny, and I would never consider the sacrifice of your youth and ardor to an old codger like me if I expected to live another ten or twenty years, but—"

Jenny's eyes opened wide, her lips parted, but no words came from between them.

"But I know as a physician that I will not," he finished calmly.

Jenny threw back the covers and crouched forward on the bed directly in front of him. "Sir Charles?" she asked imploringly.

"It is not quite the same but a similar condition to your mother's, Jenny; the progress of the disease is slower, more gradual. It is why I left London five years ago. My work had been my life, but I was no longer capable of coping with anything but a limited country practice."

"Did Mama know?"

"That we would not be separated too long?" His face seemed to be lit from within. "Yes, Jenny, she knew."

"How long?" mumbled Jenny.

"A few years, which is why I permit myself the selfishness of asking you to brighten my life," he smiled cheerfully, amending, "what is left of my life for that short while. You were the joy of your mother's existence. I am asking you for a few years to be the joy of mine. In doing so you will help me keep my promise to her."

Jenny put a tentative hand on his arm. He felt it quivering even as she said in a quiet, steady voice, "Dear Sir Charles, I would be honored to become Lady Melville."

Clarendon Hotel
London
18th September 1865

My dear Sir Lewis,

I have the great pleasure of informing you that this morning your daughter

Janet and I were united in wedlock by the Reverend Timothy Hawkins of a neighboring parish. Out of respect for your recent bereavement, we were married by special license in a quiet, private ceremony.

Felicitations may be addressed to Lady Melville at our home in Brighton, where we both prefer to live.

We are staying on in London for several days, however, so that I may attend to some business affairs, including the settlement of twenty thousand pounds, which I propose to make on your daughter. She will, of course, have more money hereafter, as my will has already been changed in her favor, and the thirty-year difference in our ages makes it more than likely that I will predecease her by several decades.

As her father, you are naturally concerned for Lady Melville's future, so I hope the knowledge of these arrangements will ease your mind. I can only conclude by saying that it will be my chief endeavor all the days of my life to make her happy.

> Yours respectfully,
> Charles Edward Melville, Bt.

"Would you like to see my letter to your father before I seal it, Jenny?" her husband asked.

She came to the desk and started reading over his shoulder.

By the second paragraph she was chuckling; by the end tears of laughter stood in her eyes.

"Sir Charles, you are a wicked man!" she told him.

"I thought that would sort him!" he said with satisfaction. "There. Ready for the penny post."

"Are you really going to give me twenty thousand pounds?" she asked naively.

"I already have. In fact, I want you to see my lawyer, Mr. Wickersham, tomorrow and start to deal directly with him, concerning your own funds. I have properties and investments, and it is important that you learn to confer competently with the men who are in charge of both and to be able in time to give them direction, too. I have always found it deplorable," he added with energy, "that women are kept in such ignorance of their husbands' affairs and turned into such weak, helpless creatures."

"You will be a wealthy widow one day, Jenny," he mentioned matter-of-factly. "The wealth will carry responsibilities as well as privileges. You will require strength, knowledge, and independence to handle both wisely. I think you are capable of all I intend for you to do."

"I will try my best not to disappoint you, Sir Charles," Lady Melville told her husband. Her solemn face and earnest voice made it a pledge and a promise.

Chapter Nine

No MATTER HOW OFTEN JANET, LADY MEL-
ville, traveled up to London—and she went
regularly to consult with her husband's lawyer, Mr. Wickersham, and his publisher, Mr.
Ellis, as well as her own man of affairs, Mr.
Otey-Powell—she never wearied of contrast-
ing the journey with the one she had suffered
through on the day she ran away from Monksdale to seek refuge with Sir Charles at
Brighton.

Her own elegant and beautifully upholstered carriage with the two dapple-gray horses that had been Sir Charles's wedding gift to
his bride conveyed Peggy and her to the railway station. Her coachman, Harvey, who did
double duty as a gardener, saw them both
safely ensconced in a first-class carriage with
a picnic basket at their feet, bountifully
packed by Mrs. Breedon to provide for their
every refreshment need. At each stage of her

trip, she was furnished with any object that affluence could offer for her comfort and every attention that the most demanding of women could have desired.

On her right hand she usually wore the opal and diamond ring and pinned to her bodice the matching brooch that Sir Charles had given her on her twenty-first birthday. The purse that dangled from her wrist always contained a thick sheaf of bills, but at the back of her mind lay the comfortable knowledge that, in the unlikely event she should run short of funds, a message to Mr. Wickersham or a note to her own man of affairs, and all the money that she desired would be promptly hers—this by Sir Charles's written order.

Her usual quarterly visit had been planned for mid-October of 1866, but when the time arrived Jenny expressed reluctance to leave home.

Sir Charles was far from strong enough to go with her, and for the first time in their thirteen months of marriage she observed a lack of health and spirits in him that disposed her to think that he was not well enough to be left.

She felt strongly inclined to postpone her journey, but when she said as much to her husband, he adamantly opposed a delay.

"The change will be good for you," he said

firmly. "I have noticed that a little trip of any sort always sets you up. I know you love Brighton, but you need the stimulation of a concert or two and the London theater. To say nothing of London restaurants." His eyes twinkled. "I told Mr. Wickersham he is to see that you have no less than two sound meals at other than a ladies' confectionary."

"Jenny, Jenny," he laughed affectionately. "Your eyes are sparkling as though I had proposed to deck you in emeralds and diamonds. Oyster patties from Saint James Hall or your mutton from Simpson's seem to do for you what jewels will do for any other woman."

"I am not any other woman," Jenny said impulsively, reaching out for his thin, veined hand. She saw with a pang of grief that he could no longer be considered stocky. "I am *your* woman and Lady Caroline's daughter."

He had strength enough to press her fingers so tightly that she cried out in pain, half real, half affected.

"Amen to that," said Sir Charles, and betwixt his laughter and her tears, discussion of a postponement was shelved. At the dinner table, when Jenny brought it up again, Sir Charles informed her phlegmatically that Peggy had already packed her bags.

"You are one stubborn man."

"Aye," said Sir Charles, with the burr he could bring into his voice at will, "it's a reputation we Scots have."

"To be plain, sir, you Scots are not so much stubborn as pig-headed. At least, will you let me leave Peggy? She knows—"

"Jenny," roared Sir Charles, "you are neither my mother nor my nanny. Now no more of this damned nonsense. You will take Peggy, and I will be well attended by Mrs. Breedon and that new maid Sayers, who," he paused and rolled a satiric eye at her, "I presume you thought I was unaware had attended the Nightingale Training School for nurses at Saint Thomas Hospital."

Jenny, who had presumed just that, retained the grace to blush, and in her confusion she pushed away from the table without so much as tasting her dessert.

"Shall we have some music?" she asked hastily as they walked toward the drawing room.

"Not if you propose to provide it, my love," he replied promptly, taking her arm. "Our good sovereign has much to answer for in making musical evenings so popular without specifying that talent is a requisite for those who perform."

"I thought *you* might play for *me*," said Jenny with dignity; then she spoiled the effect by sticking out her tongue at him.

So Sir Charles sat down to the piano, started off sentimentally with *The Last Rose of Summer*, and then went directly to one of the rollicking sea chanties they both loved best, Jenny joining him in the chorus where volume rather than voice created the best effect.

Toward the end of the third song, Jenny noted that her husband's fine baritone was a bit hoarse and breathy, and she came to put her arms around him from behind and rest her head a moment on his shoulder.

"That's enough for tonight, I think," she told him. "Shall I read to you now? At least you approve of my reading voice." She tried to sound teasing when she would rather have wept.

Sir Charles crossed the room to look over some books that lay on the table. "I should like to get started on *The Mill on the Floss*," he agreed.

They sat down together on the sofa, and Jenny commenced reading, becoming so absorbed in the book herself that it was some time before she noticed that her husband had fallen asleep.

She continued to read, more softly, almost monotonously, fearful to wake him by sudden silence, until her own voice got ragged and she finally let it trail away.

Two days later, when she left for London, Sir Charles appeared to be in good shape.

With great strength of will, Jenny refrained from worrying him with directions, admonitions, or even her own fears. Only to Miss Sayers, the nurse in the guise of a maid, did she permit herself to say, "If there is the slightest change for the worse—if he needs me—if—"

"I will telegraph you at your hotel, ma'am, Lady Melville," said the patient Sayers, who had heard it all before.

In London, Jenny proceeded at once to her appointment with the publisher, Mr. Ellis, bearing the completed manuscript of Sir Charles's new book, *Our Bodies, Our Minds*.

Mr. Ellis, a tall, desiccated-looking man, whose only passion in life was for books, literally trembled with delight as he took the weighty manuscript from her hands into his own.

"This book will mark a milestone in medical learning if only the second half is as exciting as the original chapters Sir Charles showed to me."

He looked at Jenny in anxious query until she confirmed, "Every bit as good."

Mr. Ellis drew a deep sigh of relief and caressed the script with crablike hands before laying it on his desk. "I foresee it one day as part of the curriculum of every doctor's training," he assured her solemnly.

He sat down behind his desk. "And now to business," he added briskly.

He was gravely disappointed to learn that Sir Charles had not actually planned a new book, but Jenny comforted him with the news that her files were bursting with papers and notebooks crammed with ideas, jottings, and practical observations, enough to fill another two or three volumes.

"I think my husband might be interested in doing a book on the adulteration of food-stuffs," she mentioned in passing, at which Mr. Ellis's face registered polite disinterest.

"Surely the Food and Drug Act of 1860 has changed all that," he observed.

"No indeed, Mr. Ellis, it has not," declared Jenny with energy. "It was a first step, but a very slight first step, no more than the admission that the problem exists. It is not being enforced. Our starving poor still drink their way to the grave because drink is cheap and can help them forget for a brief while the misery of their existence. The very same beer they drink can also wipe out their existence. As often as not, it has poisonous additions that can convulse the digestive tract, paralyze the nervous system, or often kill. The upper classes do no better," she continued earnestly. "They eat their way from cradle to grave, often as not, prematurely. Dirty cows in filthy byres produce contaminated milk. The good wheat content is still being milled out of bread and dangerous alum added. Lead is a common ingredient—"

She broke off abruptly. "Forgive me, I did not mean to lecture, but my husband has imbued me with some of his strong feelings on this subject. The truth is, we English commit suicide with poisoned foodstuffs every day of our lives."

"Bravo!" applauded Mr. Ellis in a deep voice, oddly at variance with his stringy frame. "If that same passionate commitment could be put in a book, I am sure it would be most effective. Of course," he added with editorial caution, "I should like to see some chapters before I commit Ellis and Company to publication."

"I will speak to my husband and communicate with you from Brighton," said Jenny, rising to shake hands.

That night she and Peggy went to a concert at Covent Garden, and the following evening Mr. Wickersham took her to supper at Fenton's in the West End, which had one of the few acceptable restaurants to which a gentleman could bring a lady.

A lady was not expected to show much appetite, but since Jenny prided herself on being a ladyship, not a lady, she astonished the waiters but not Mr. Wickersham, who had dined with her before and knew her capacity. Since it matched his own—he always seemed to be bursting out of his white satin waistcoat —they always dined together most agreeably.

Jenny could not help thinking with some merriment—as she worked her way through the soup, the fish, the venison, the removes, and the side dishes, and then made dainty use of the finger bowl in preparation for the fruit, the ices, and the pastry—of her impassioned speech to Mr. Ellis on overeating the day before.

"But this is a special treat," she excused herself aloud.

"I beg your pardon, dear Lady Melville?" Mr. Wickersham was slightly hard of hearing and thought he had missed the earlier part of her speech.

"I said that since I don't eat like this at home—you are giving me a special treat—I am not really being *too* greedy."

"Certainly not," Mr. Wickersham reassured her. "And you certainly do not—er—your form —you are not overly endowed with flesh—er— that is—" He was gazing at the décolletage of her burgundy velvet gown with silver bugle trim, which plainly exposed the upper curve of her most obvious endowments. "You are— er—quite small-waisted and er—"

The poor man was sweating profusely. Jenny took pity on him. "Thank you, Mr.

Wickersham. The meal was delicious. If you will excuse me for a few moments."

She stood up, thereby elevating her décolletage well above his eye level, and shook out her skirts. As she walked sedately out of the dining room, she was convulsed with laughter.

When she returned a few minutes later, a silvery chiffon scarf was draped carelessly about her neck and shoulders in such a way as to spare poor plump Mr. Wickersham provocation. She sat down opposite him and said, "Now, about your plans for the Sussex line stocks, Mr. Wickersham," and the business atmosphere was soon reestablished.

Her last appointment before leaving London was with Mr. Otey-Powell, her astute, middle-aged man of affairs, who had done well by her in investments, though she did not feel personally drawn to him.

They went over the list of her stocks, Jenny asking questions about sales and purchases, briefly approving or making notes for further study.

"I am pleased to say your shipping stock is doing well. I have some thoughts of increasing your investment in Cunard," Mr. Otey-Powell told her in conclusion with pompous self-congratulation. It was he, not Jenny, who had pushed the most for the purchase of her shipping stock.

She considered their conference to be over and stood up, ready to bid him good-bye. A single added sentence froze her to the floor.

"I have decided," Mr. Otey-Powell informed her, "against investing any of your funds in Irish Rose."

Chapter Ten

23rd October, 1866

Dear Lady Melville,

Pursuant to your directions, after our discussion of the Irish Rose shipping firm, I conducted a thorough investigation and hereby append my report on the history of the company and a list of pertinent figures.

It is my considered opinion—in which I am sure you will concur after surveying the report and figures—that, at this time, any money put into Irish Rose would be at risk.

I will, of course, in view of your interest, keep in touch with the situation and advise you of any change.

Yours respectfully,
Mortimer Otey-Powell

The moment the bulky envelope had arrived from Mr. Otey-Powell, Jenny seized on it and rushed off to the garden. It was a brisk autumn day, and she shivered a little, having forgotten to throw a shawl over her leaf-green promenade gown.

The letter, after a hasty reading, fell to her feet along with the financial statement. She held onto the pages marked "Personal Report" as though they might run away from her if she let go.

As she began to read, she unconsciously stroked the ruffled organdy layers of her collar. Underneath it lay the pink pearl necklace that she wore always against her skin in the day hours when her dresses were buttoned to the throat.

Report on the Irish Rose Shipping Line

The Irish Rose operates as a modest merchant trading venture. It was begun in 1863 with the purchase of one small schooner by David Philip Fenton. Mr. Fenton, who was then a captain on active service in Her Majesty's navy, negotiated through a Liverpool agent, E. F. Harbuck.

It is believed but not known for sure that the funds used for the original Irish Rose enterprise were supplied in part by the young man, in part by a loan from his uncle, Lord William Carroll, Earl of Denby. (Mr. Fenton is in line to the title after Lord William and his two sons.)

In early 1864, after the purchase of his third vessel, Captain Fenton resigned from the navy and removed to Liverpool to personally direct the operation of the Irish Rose.

By late 1865, through shrewd trading and daring enterprise, Mr. Fenton had laid the foundation for his own personal fortune and the great expansion of the Irish Rose line. In mid-1863, immediately after securing his first vessel, backing his purchase with all that he owned, he bought up large supplies of rosin and turpentine. As the American Civil War progressed, these two articles were in desperate need across the Atlantic. Mr. Fenton warehoused his stores in Liverpool for some time, selling at the strategic moment to realize an enormous profit.

As of this January of 1866, the Irish Rose line comprised six vessels . . .

Jenny turned eagerly to the second page of the report, and for the first time in years a half-forgotten expression came breathlessly from between her lips. "Oh, my!" said Jenny, Lady Melville, tears filling up her eyes.

When her eyes were clear again, she read the words once more.

. . . the Irish Rose line comprised six vessels: the *Thistledown*, the *Queen's High*, the *Dumpling*, the *Pink Pearl*, the *First Waltz*, and the *Sweet Jenny*.

Mr. Fenton was also elected to the Liverpool Town Council and this year has been appointed to serve on the Mersey Docks and Harbour Board.

Personal note from Mr. Otey-Powell:

This past winter—in January and February to be precise—I gave serious consideration to putting some of your funds into the Irish Rose, not for immediate profit but as a sound investment for the future. Since then, however, there has been a very disturbing turn of events. Captain Sawyer of the *Sweet Jenny*—the pride of the Irish Rose line, its largest ship, and the one with the greatest record of profit—took it across the Atlantic to South America on a spring voyage and never returned. He sold the cargo illegally and used the money obtained for personal trade, again for his own benefit.

Captain Sawyer is an old friend of Mr. Fenton's from his navy days—they served together for several years—and he has obviously been trusted not wisely but too well to put him in the incredible position of being able to steal the chief ship of the line.

Mr. Fenton's speedy knowledge of Captain Sawyer's plans seem to have come from the first mate of the *Sweet Jenny*, Eddy Ramsay, also a former navy seaman. (It would seem Mr. Fenton has a personal interest there, too, because he put up money to get Ramsay out of the navy.)

I shall look for Eddy Ramsay and be very good to him—for your sake—if he gets on my ship.

The news about the *Sweet Jenny* has circulated all over Liverpool and London trading circles, casting great doubts on the credibility of Mr. Fenton and the soundness of the Irish Rose line.

The stock has fallen off. Investors have withdrawn. Trading deals are being canceled.

Mr. Fenton has backed the line with his own private fortune, and he, perhaps, may be able to save it, but no sound business man could advise an investment in Irish Rose at this time.

Telegraph message from Lady Janet Melville to Mr. Mortimer Otey-Powell:

BUY ALL THE IRISH ROSE STOCK OBTAINABLE.

Telegraph message from Mr. Mortimer Otey-Powell to Lady Charles Melville:

I MUST STRONGLY ADVISE YOU AGAINST YOUR DECISION. STOCK UNSOUND.

Telegraph message from Lady Melville to Mr. Mortimer Otey-Powell:

YOUR ADVICE NOTED. NOW BUY AS DIRECTED.

Telegraph message from Mr. M. Otey-Powell to Sir Charles Melville:

PLEASE INTERCEDE WITH YOUR WIFE TO DIS-COURAGE RASH DECISION TO BUY IRISH ROSE STOCK.

Telegraph message from Sir Charles Melville to Mr. Mortimer Otey-Powell:

AS PREVIOUSLY DIRECTED, BUY IRISH ROSE STOCK AT ONCE.

Letter from Janet, Lady Melville, to Mr. Mortimer Otey-Powell:

Sir:

As my confidential man of affairs, I consider that you have committed a gross breach of faith in approaching my husband to intercede on a business matter that was being conducted between yourself and me.

Please deliver all papers relating to my business affairs into the hands of Mr. Clarence Wickersham, attorney, Gray's Inn Court, who will personally appear at your office to accept them, with all necessary affidavits of release.

Since you appear to believe a woman incapable of making any business judgment without recourse to male sanction, you should be pleased to know that this move has Sir Charles's full approval.

Letter from Mr. Clarence Wickersham to Lady Janet Melville the day after Christmas of 1866:

I have the most glorious news for you, if you have not already read of it in the newspapers by the time this missive arrives.

The Sweet Jenny is in anchorage in Liverpool, restored to the Irish Rose line and carrying a rich cargo to boot.

Shipping circles across England are resounding with the story. The rightful owner, Mr. David Fenton, bearing the necessary papers of ownership, took a daring and courageous four-month voyage to recover it, first traveling across the Atlantic, where he arrived at the port of New Orleans. He then transversed the Isthmus of Darien and continued his journey up the Pacific Coast until he reached the city of San Francisco barely hours ahead of the nefarious Captain Sawyer's plan to take the Sweet Jenny across the Pacific to the Orient, from where it is unlikely that the ship would ever have been recovered.

Captain Fenton boarded the Sweet Jenny in San Francisco port, with the proper American authorities and the ship's first mate E. Ramsay to support his claim.

This bold personal rescue of his ship, with its attendant publicity, has had the most marvelous effect upon Mr. Fenton's standing in the business community, both here and abroad; as a result of which, the price for Irish Rose stock has soared to an amazing level. At this writing, the upward trend continues.

If you wish to sell, you will be a very rich woman. May I know your intention?

Telegraph from Lady Melville to Mr. Charles Wickersham:

MY THANKS FOR YOUR KIND LETTER. MY INTENTION IS NOT TO SELL IRISH ROSE. I REPEAT. DO NOT ON ANY ACCOUNT SELL. WISHING YOU A HAPPY AND PROSPEROUS NEW YEAR.

Personal Report on David Fenton from the office of Mr. Clarence Wickersham to Sir Charles Melville:

Mr. Fenton is unmarried. In recent years his name was seriously linked with that of the eldest daughter of Lord Beckwith. The lady, however, married Sir Hugh Rickles earlier this year. Mr. Fenton has also been frequently in the company of Miss Clara Summerhouse, heiress to a Liverpool shipping fortune, but a marriage is no longer expected since his long voyage to America, during which the lady started looking elsewhere.

For the past three years he has had the same mistress in keeping, an actress named Sheila Dale, who came originally from the Scotland Road area of Liverpool but now lives in a pleasant house near Walton, which is registered in Mr. Fenton's name though he lodges in an apartment over his Mersey offices.

When he visits London, which he does usually twice a year attending to business matters, he visits the same lady, a Mrs. Maxwell, in her villa in Richmond. It appears to be an amiable but not exclusive arrangement, as it is no secret that Mrs. Maxwell has other admirers. Many other admirers.

Post Scriptum in letter of commitment from Mr. Bernard Ellis of Ellis and Company, Publishers, to Sir Charles Melville:

It will be noted in the contract that in the event of your disability or death, it is acceptable to us that your wife continue with the manuscript of "Let Us Eat Poison." You were quite correct, sir. I could not distinguish between the chapters written exclusively by you or those that were composed by Lady Melville. My congratulations, dear sir, on such incredible teamwork. This book is indeed a public service. I predict it will change the nature of food processing and consumption.

Telegraph from Clarence Wickersham to Lady Melville:

AS ONE OF LARGEST INVESTORS IN IRISH ROSE, DO YOU WISH TO ATTEND IMPORTANT SHARE-HOLDERS' MEETING IN LIVERPOOL ON 10TH MARCH, 1867?

Telegraph from Lady Melville to Mr. Wickersham:

NO. MY STRICT ANONYMITY IS TO BE PRE-SERVED. CONTINUE PRESENT POLICY OF AN-SWERING ALL INQUIRIES. TO WIT: YOU HOLD THE SHARES AS ATTORNEY IN FACT FOR AN UNDISCLOSED OWNER. PLEASE KEEP ME AD-VISED.

Telegraph from C. Wickersham in Liverpool to Lady Melville:

SHAREHOLDERS' MEETING CANCELED BECAUSE OF EXTREME TRAGEDY IN CARROLL FAMILY. THE EARL, COUNTESS, AND BOTH SONS KILLED IN HORRENDOUS RAILWAY ACCIDENT ON WAY UP TO SCOTLAND TO ATTEND WEDDING OF YOUNG-ER SON. FENTON NOW EARL OF DENBY.

Chapter Eleven

JENNY MOVED RESTLESSLY AGAINST THE CUSH-
ions of Sir Lewis Rosellen's handsome crested
carriage.

"Catherine might have sent something
more comfortable than a farm gig for Peggy
and Miss Sayers."

"They were not nearly as surprised or dis-
tressed as you, my dear," her husband observed sardonically. "The comfort of those
who serve them has never been an over-
whelming preoccupation of the English upper
classes."

Distracted—as he had meant her to be—
Jenny made a wry face at him.

"Yes, you—you Scot, that's perfectly true,
but must you always remind me?"

A moment later she reverted to the real
cause of her fretfulness.

"I don't see why you insisted that we come,"

she burst out for perhaps the eighth or ninth time that day. "It's been such a tiring journey for you, and Nell—Lady Eleanor—would have understood."

"From the way you have always described her, I feel sure Lady Eleanor would be most understanding," Sir Charles returned calmly. "At such a time of grief, however, I am also certain she will need all the friends she has about her. You *were* her good friend?"

"Say, rather, *she* was *mine*," Jenny declared in her old impetuous way. "Despite the difference in our ages—she had her coming out at the same time as Catherine—she was always so kind to me, so—so understanding," she faltered.

She looked at her husband with some concern, not knowing how to continue. Even in a marriage such as theirs, it did not seem either tactful or appropriate to finish her sentence.

So understanding when I fell in love with David.

Sir Charles reached out to clasp her hand. Once that same touch had been a source of warmth and comfort to her. More lately the wasted strength of his hand warned her of his near mortality.

She would not think about it. Determinedly, she forced a cheerful smile and put her face against the window.

"We are almost there. Another half-mile will bring us to the gates of the Abbey."

Suddenly she gave a convulsive little shiver. She had been so busy dwelling on the tragedy to the Carrolls and her worry over Sir Charles, she had not spared much thought for this return to the home where she had spent the first eighteen years of her life.

With that uncanny perception so characteristic of him, Sir Charles put his arm around her, gently stroking her shoulder.

"Jenny, you are not the frightened little girl who ran away from Monksdale. You are Lady Melville of Brighton, lovely, rich, important Lady Melville, who writes books, trains with her husband as a nurse, and conducts her own business affairs so astutely as to have made a fortune unaided."

With a tired sigh, she leaned more comfortably against him.

"Dear, dear Sir Charles, you are right. I almost forgot." She straightened up, tossing her hair back—her Irish foxfire hair. *Hold your head high like a queen, Jenny.* "I shall not forget again."

It proved impossible not to remember and draw a mental contrast with the past when her father and Catherine, as well as her brother-in-law, welcomed her with every appearance of cordiality, showing her all the deference and courtesy due an honored guest. Such treatment had never been accorded her in the old days. To Sir Charles, they were not merely warm and welcoming but almost obsequious.

Sir Charles and Lady Melville, Jenny reflected to herself in quite her husband's sardonic manner as they all sat down to tea together and the barrage of complimentary commentaries continued. Rich, powerful relations.

"Have you seen Lady Eleanor yet?" she asked Catherine at the first opportunity.

"Yesterday afternoon. She looked utterly wretched. Poor Nell. Black never did become her. She could not leave off crying to speak sensibly. With her red eyes and swollen face, all draped in crape, she was a sorry sight."

In her mind, Jenny slowly counted to five, then said as mildly as possible, "Losing one's entire family in a single day is hardly conducive to good looks."

"You are so right, dear Lady Melville," said Henry Rosellen with a sharp glance at his wife. "Precisely what Catherine meant, is it not, my dear?"

My God, thought Jenny, another version of Sir Lewis. As though one wasn't bad enough.

"Lord David," said the gentleman so slandered in his daughter's mind, "was paying his cousin every imaginable attention. Her care seemed to be his chief concern, just as it should be. A very proper attitude."

"Very proper, indeed," echoed Henry Rosellen.

Jenny looked over at her father in astonishment. Lord David. The title rolled off his lips as though he had been using it forever. The praise, too. What extraordinary self-delusion, she marveled, not doubting for a moment that he had conveniently forgotten the time when that same lord was shown the door of Monksdale Abbey, his proposal spurned, his suit pronounced unworthy of consideration.

The funeral took place the next day, and the new earl had been foresighted enough to have half a dozen members of the local constabulary outside the churchyard, where the row of four gaping graves lay exposed. With interest spurred by lurid newspaper accounts, gawkers had come from nearby villages and as far away as London to witness the exciting sight of four members of the nobility dead and buried together.

Back at Carroll house, Jenny finally got the chance to kiss and embrace Lady Eleanor. "Dear Nell, how sorry I am," she whispered. "My heart goes out to you."

Lady Eleanor hugged her convulsively.

"Thank you, Jenny, and thank you for coming." Her lips quivered; she began to cry again.

It was true that black crape and red, swollen eyes did not become Nell, thought Jenny with compassion, her own eyes welling up, any more than they would have become anyone under like conditions.

Unable to offer platitudes in the face of such grief, she could only hold and pat her weeping friend, murmuring disjointedly, "There, Nell, dear Nell."

Someone approached them from behind Jenny. A well-remembered voice, brusque with concern, said, "Nell, this is too much for you. Why do you not go to your room and try to rest?"

Jenny turned around to face him, with Nell still clinging to her arm.

All the color left David's face at the sight of her.

"A very good notion, Lord David," Jenny said almost composedly. "You are right. This commotion is too much for Lady Eleanor to bear."

Lady Eleanor's husband, Sir Harry Langley was evidently of the same mind. He excused himself from several of the funeral guests by pointing them in the direction of refreshments and came over to escort his weeping wife upstairs.

"You look wonderful, Jenny," said the new Earl of Denby.

Jenny could not help remembering the last

time the two of them had stood alone in a sea of people in this very room. She had not looked wonderful to him then. She had looked, in words of his that had haunted her for longer than she cared to remember, "hideously thin and haggard."

The old bitter need to throw those words back in his face no longer tormented her. As Sir Charles had pointed out, thought Jenny with serene confidence, she was Lady Melville now, lovely, rich, talented Lady Melville.

"Thank you, Lord David," said Jenny quietly.

"Ah, no, not you too, Jenny," he said with sudden bitterness. Then, seeing her bewilderment, he shrugged, pitching his voice higher in a cynical parody of sycophantic respect. "Good morning, my lord. How d'you do, your lordship? Lord William is dead, long live Lord David."

Stung, that this was intended for her, Jenny cried, "I care no more about titles than I ever did!"

"Yet you are Lady Melville with a rich husband thirty years older."

"You think that is why I married him?" The look Jenny flashed him was full of scorn and pity. "Then you do not know me, and what is more, Lord David, you never did."

"What else was I to think?"

"Why, anything but the obvious," she said

lightly. "Would you like to meet my husband? He is standing there, across the room, the one with his hand on the mantle."

"Good God, Jenny!" he cried out in accents of extreme revulsion, manners forgotten in amazement. "It is worse even than I thought. That gray-beard; why, he looks old enough to be your grandfather."

"Not quite," Jenny said softly. "He is only tired from the journey. And my grandfather was the finest gentleman I ever knew—until Sir Charles."

"Are you telling me that you are happy with him, Jenny?"

"Do you know," she said thoughtfully, "I never thought about it or asked myself that question before. The answer is yes. I have been very happy with him. Except for one short period of my life," she added, looking squarely into the dark, brooding eyes across from her, and he knew well what period it was she referred to, "I have never been happier."

"Sir Charles is a man of depth and breadth. I refer to his mental qualities, you understand," she added playfully. "As a physician, he has done more to help his fellow man, I would warrant, than all the rest of this assemblage put together. He has intelligence, vision, humor—and, remember, I came from a home where these were qualities to be suppressed. He opened new worlds to me. I knew nothing. I *was* nothing. I—he—"

"My God, Jenny, you love him?" he asked incredulously.

"With all my heart."

Chapter Twelve

JENNY SHUDDERED AWAY FROM THE SIGHT OF the great ugly mausoleum.

"Mama is just beyond," she said to Sir Charles, "next to my infant brother."

He stood erect before the grave while Jenny went down on her knees to place a great armful of mixed spring flowers across the grassy mound and carefully crop a few limp weeds.

The headstone, a plain marble slab, read "Lady Caroline, Beloved Wife of Sir Lewis Rosellen. Beloved Mother of Catherine, Margaret, and Janet." And the dates.

Seeing the wintery smile on Sir Charles's face, Jenny clutched at his arm.

"Remember what you said to me once, dear Sir Charles, it's only a body from which the spirit has flown. Well, this is only a piece of stone with meaningless words inscribed. The true ones are engraved on both our hearts.

Lady Caroline Conroy, Beloved of Sir Charles Melville."

"Thank you, Jenny." The twisted smile melted into tenderness as she slipped her arm through his and their hands clasped together. He looked down at the grave. She might have been standing there, Jenny thought. The look in his eyes was the one he used to give her alone.

"Caroline," he repeated. "Caroline, beloved of Charles."

"I have been very stupid," Jenny said in a small, remorseful voice as they walked slowly back toward Monksdale. "I should have known why you wanted to come to Somersetshire for the funeral."

He felt no need to answer but just pressed her arm closer to his side. Their thoughtful, understanding silence lasted till they reached the Abbey.

On the day before their return to Brighton, they paid their last call at Carroll House. Lady Eleanor was resting upstairs and sent a message by her maid asking Jenny to go up to her.

Sir Charles joined the rest of the callers in the drawing room, selecting an isolated arm chair in one corner and studying the throng of guests around Lord David with hooded eyes and a slightly cynical smile.

Despite his courteous attention to those

around him, Lord David was not unaware of the penetrating stare from across the room.

Presently, he broke free and by degrees made his way across to the older man.

"May I offer you some refreshment, sir? I am," he hesitated, "David Fenton."

Sir Charles bowed his head slightly in acknowledgment. "I was aware, Lord David," he said agreeably. "May I introduce myself— Charles Melville?"

Lord David made a stiff little bow. "I, too, was aware, Sir Charles," he retorted, unable to keep the hurt and bitterness out of his voice. "Jenny's husband."

"Jenny's husband—to be sure." Sir Charles fingered the graying beard his host had found so objectionable the previous week. "Yes, I have that privilege for a short while."

"S-sir?" David stammered, a little taken aback by this unusual remark.

Sir Charles stood up. "I believe you mentioned some refreshment, my lord," he said amiably. "I am sure you must have some excellent Madeira in the library—or perhaps your study—any private place will do."

Lord David's brows lifted a fraction. Then he said courteously, "Please come with me, Sir Charles. My uncle did keep a very fine Madeira in his library."

He led the way out of the drawing room, pausing now and then to acknowledge a greeting, an outstretched hand, a murmur of sympathy, a message for Lady Eleanor.

Outside the door of the library, he told a young footman, "I am not to be disturbed."

Inside the library two glasses of Madeira were poured before either of them spoke.

Sir Charles accepted his wine. "Thank you, Lord David." He tasted it and pronounced, "Ah, yes, an excellent Madeira."

Lord David, impatient of these prolonged courtesies, asked bluntly, "You wished to be private with me, sir?"

"Why, yes." Sir Charles swirled the wine gently in his glass. "I thought it best since I intend to be—perhaps—a bit impertinent."

"I beg your pardon?"

"I am afraid I may have to beg yours before I am done. Most men do not care to have their private affairs explored by a stranger."

"I take it," Lord David said somewhat grimly, "that you have been exploring mine?"

Sir Charles smiled gently. "I am afraid so."

"May I ask to what end, sir?" Lord David was obviously holding his temper in check with great effort.

"To Jenny's happiness."

"Jenny?"

"Jenny. My wife. Her happiness means everything to me—both now and after I am gone."

"After you—are you—" Lord David broke off

147

in midsentence. Even in such an extraordinary conversation, certain conventions must be preserved. One did not ask a virtual stranger if he was about to die.

Sir Charles laughed out loud, having followed his host's thinking processes with remarkable precision.

"Yes, Lord David, I am," he said, still chuckling a bit. "No later than this time next year—probably a bit sooner—my Jenny will be a very rich widow."

Condolences seemed out of place and not in question.

"You have a reason for confiding in me, I presume?"

"I am not concerned with your mistresses, so we may leave Mrs. Maxwell and Sheila Dale out of this discussion," said Lord David's extraordinary guest. "There is, however, the Beckwith girl, now Lady Rickles, and Clara Summerhouse. I was unable to discover, Lord David, if you were the pursuer or the pursued."

Lord David crossed his arms. "Were you, indeed?" he said with a sardonic sympathy worthy of Sir Charles. "Well, if it is any of your affair, sir—and you seem to have made my affairs your concern—I should say it was a little of both. Why, may I ask, must you know?"

"If you wanted another woman, then you

may no longer want Jenny—in which case I am wasting both my time and yours, and I have only to apologize and take my leave of you." Sir Charles inclined his head in a gracious bow. "Shall I?"

David set his glass down on a serving table, spilling half the contents. He did not take advantage of Sir Charles's offer but sat down in a leather arm chair and stared at a row of bookshelves for several minutes. "I am not a monk, sir. And I am unmarried. By choice. I have wanted many women, but I have only once wished to have one for wife—or for life."

"Jenny?"

"Jenny."

"The fortune-hunters will be after her." Sir Charles set his glass down, too, but without any mishap. "You needn't fear about them," he said with pride. "My Jenny has a shrewd head on her shoulders; she is a good judge of a man's sincerity. She will mourn me for a while," he told Lord David quite seriously, "but she should not be left to mourn too long."

"Are you giving me your blessing, Sir Charles?"

The satirical note in his voice was wasted. "Yes," said the gray-bearded baronet to the young earl. "With three provisions, I am. If you can make her happy, make her love you, and make her forgive you."

"Forgive *me*?"

"I dare say you thought the shoe was on the other foot," observed Sir Charles dispassionately, going toward the library door. "Well, well, it will give you something to reflect about this winter while you wait to read my obituary in the *Times*."

Lord David hurried to open the door for him, and Sir Charles turned and held out his hand to the younger man.

"I condole with you on your loss, Lord David. From what Jenny has said, you would prefer to be minus both titles and estates and have your aunt and uncle and cousins alive."

"Much rather," said Lord David curtly after their brief handshake.

"To be chairman of the Irish Rose line, through your own effort and achievement, is a worthy enough endeavor for any man."

"Is there anything you do not know, sir?" David asked him in bewildered astonishment.

"Many things," Sir Charles chuckled. "Principally, how to get hold of the fountain of youth." He clapped Lord David on the shoulder. "I bid you good-bye, Captain Fenton. Be good to my Jenny or I will haunt you."

Chapter Thirteen

"IT IS A SIMPLE, STRAIGHTFORWARD WILL, Lady Melville," said Mr. Wickersham approvingly, "and I believe you are fully acquainted with all the terms?"

She was still nodding agreement when he began to enumerate them.

"Fifteen hundred pounds to your housekeeper, Mrs. Breedon, and the same amount to the housemaid, Peggy Newton, in gratitude for her services to your dear mother. To all other servants in his employ, one hundred for each year of service or fraction thereof. Five hundred to his nurse, Lillian Sayers, and the same to a half-dozen hospitals and nursing schools. Five thousand each for his cousins Tom MacWilliams and Hector MacWilliams of Edinburgh, the same for his cousin Jean Melville Gordon of Glasgow. All else, both monies and properties, to be yours, free and clear, nothing held in trust.

"My dear Lady Melville. Such faith he had in your good sense and business acumen—permit me to say, not without reason." He took off his spectacles and carefully wiped the lenses. "Dear me!" he said. "I shall miss him sorely. Such a fine man. Always a smile or jest. I do have these fussy ways, and how he loved to tease me about them. Kindly, you understand," he assured her hastily. "He was always kind."

"I know," said Jenny.

"'Feed my wife up,' he would say, every time you came to town. 'Send her back to me round and plump, she is fading away.' It was just his jest, you understand," he said earnestly to Jenny.

"I know," answered Jenny, looking down at her lap, where her hands lay convulsively clasped.

"I am to be executor of the will," Mr. Wickersham continued, carefully fitting his spectacles back over the bridge of his nose.

"Yes, I know," said Jenny faintly.

"So honored by his trust," he murmured, and this time she merely nodded.

Peggy came into the room. "You sent for me, ma'am—sir?" she asked doubtfully.

"Your mistress is tired and should lie down on her bed," said Mr. Wickersham, "but first it is my pleasant duty to inform you, Peggy, that

Sir Charles remembered you most generously in his will. You are to have fifteen hundred pounds."

For a moment Peggy was struck dumb.

Then she repeated in dazed accents, "Fifteen hun-dred. Lord have mercy!"

She plumped herself down on a chair, trying to absorb the news, and was only galvanized into rising by Mr. Wickersham's shocked look.

Lady Melville wound up leading her maid upstairs to rest rather than the other way around, but not before she had said to Mr. Wickersham, "In addition to being Sir Charles's executor, I hope you are willing to continue to manage my affairs, sir."

As she and Peggy mounted the steps, she could still hear him twittering in Sir Charles's study. "So honored. So kind. Oh, dear."

Soon after Mr. Wickersham withdrew to dress for dinner, Miss Sayers, the nurse, originally smuggled into the household as a housemaid, sought an interview with Jenny in her sitting room.

"I was wondering, Lady Melville," she asked, with all the confidence of her new-found fortune of five hundred pounds, "just when you wished me to leave."

"Not at all, Miss Sayers, if you are willing to stay on."

"I would rather not be a housemaid again, ma'am," Miss Sayers said diffidently. "As a temporary strategem, to induce Sir Charles to have me in your household, I was willing, but—." Her voice faded away apologetically.

"No housemaiding," Jenny said briskly. "I envisioned you more as our head nurse. We would need two others, I believe—that would be up to you. I will be only part-time help to you. I have to finish Sir Charles's books, and, of course, I am not fully trained; you would still have to teach me."

"Whatever are you planning, Lady Melville?" gasped Miss Sayers. "Surely not a hospital?"

"This is my home, and I love it," said Jenny, seemingly at tangent. "I do not want to leave. Still, it is far too big a house for one woman alone with a handful of servants. No, not a hospital, Miss Sayers, more in the nature of a—a way station—a stopping-off place for perhaps six to eight people, whom the hospitals cannot help, people with wasting sicknesses of the nervous or muscular systems, like my husband and mother, people who need comfort and care and kindness during their last months and years."

She smiled up at the nurse. "Please sit down, Miss Sayers, and tell me what you think. Would you be agreeable to staying on as head nurse?"

"Oh, gracious, I certainly would, Lady Melville."

"My own plan is to take over the west wing as my private residence. The rest of the house could be converted to use for our—recovery home, shall we call it?"

"Perhaps convalescing home, ma'am?" Miss Sayers suggested.

"Excellent. Convalescing home it shall be. Will two other nurses be enough?"

They were still discussing their plans with great gusto when Mr. Wickersham joined them for dinner and was—for the first time— made acquainted with his client's scheme.

"Dear me! A conception worthy of Sir Charles. And to bear his name, too. The Charles Melville Convalescing Home."

He was forced once again to remove the spectacles from his nose and polish the blurred lenses with his handkerchief. "My dear Lady Melville. So noble. So worthy. Your husband would be proud."

Their planning discussion continued all through the meal. It was decided that Mr. Wickersham's first duty on returning to London would be to look into obtaining the services of an architect, one familiar with hospital design and willing to work with Lady Melville and Miss Sayers on the renovations to Melville House.

Time enough, after the renovations were set

in motion, for the selection of additional nurses, household help, and, lastly, the patients to be cared for.

"Shall you charge any fees?" Mr. Wickersham asked at one point, and Miss Sayers, too, turned in her chair to look an inquiry at Jenny.

Jenny had already given consideration to this question. "Where it cannot be afforded, our service will be free," she told them crisply. "Patients who can afford fees will be charged according to their means, especially if they are wealthy." She smiled a little. "I do not mean to discriminate against the rich. They can be sick and unwanted, too, you know."

Miss Sayers just glowed her answer, but Mr. Wickersham was heard to murmur, "So like dear Sir Charles. Oh, dear me, so good, so kind."

As he removed his spectacles again, Jenny rose hastily, signaling to Miss Sayers, and the two of them, in mercy, left him to his wine.

The next morning, before his departure for London, Jenny and Mr. Wickersham were closeted alone in the study where she and Sir Charles had worked together on his books.

The attorney was all business now.

"As soon as I receive the revised contracts from your publisher, I will forward them for your signature."

Jenny nodded. "Remind Mr. Ellis that I want a year to complete both books and that the title page is to read 'By Sir Charles Melville with the assistance of Lady Melville.'"

Mr. Wickersham made a careful note. "It will be incorporated in the contract.

"I shall send you word," he continued, "as soon as I have any architects you might seriously contemplate hiring. Would you wish me to make the final choice, or will—"

Seeing Jenny shake her head, he interrupted himself, his head cocked to one side, waiting for her to speak.

"I think it would be best if Miss Sayers and I journeyed up to London to conduct the final interviews," she said firmly. "After all, we will be the ones who have to work with him."

"A wise decision." He made another careful note.

Jenny rose. "I think we have covered everything, Mr. Wickersham, except my warmest thanks and enduring gratitude for all your assistance. Let me order the carriage now so you will not be late for your train."

The carriage ordered, Mr. Wickersham agreed to one last glass of wine.

While he was drinking it, he said with some embarrassment, "There is just one more thing, Lady Melville. Some time ago—nearly a year, I believe—Sir Charles entrusted me with a small packet for you to be given to you after his death. I did not bring it with me when I came five days ago," he coughed apologetically, "because I was under the impression—it appeared to be—in short, I thought I was attending my regular monthly business session with dear Sir Charles rather than his deathbed."

"Do you know what is in the packet?" Jenny asked him, more surprised than inquisitive.

"A manuscript, I believe. Would you wish me to send it to Brighton by one of my clerks?"

"Oh, I dare say my curiosity will survive Her Majesty's mails," Jenny told him matter-of-factly as they walked to the waiting carriage.

She stood on the steps, waving him off, a slight, gallant figure in her unrelieved black. As the carriage turned out of the driveway, hiding her from his view, Mr. Wickersham settled back against the cushions, all his thoughts taken up with the newmade widow.

Unlike most women, reflected the attorney, who was seldom given to such flights of fancy, with her magnificent red hair and buttermilk skin and the queenly way she carried herself, mourning became Lady Melville.

Chapter Fourteen

THE PACKET LEFT IN MR. WICKERSHAM'S
charge contained a manuscript and a letter.
With shaking hands, Jenny slit the seal of a
slim envelope addressed to her in her husband's hand.

My dearest Jenny,

*Life offered me no greater gift than
your mother's love. To have had yours,
too—however different a love—is more
than any one man could have a right to
expect.*

*You have cherished and cared for me,
as you did my dear Caroline. You have
worked with me as well as for me and
honored me more than I can say with
your trust and devotion.*

It has been my joy to see you grow from

a frightened, unsure girl with no belief in her own beauty, into a poised, elegant, serene, and confidently beautiful woman, worthy of any man in this kingdom.

You were never meant to live alone, Jenny. When the time comes, choose wisely and well, and do not allow injured pride to be a factor in that choice.

I do not—as you know—believe in heaven, any more than I do in hell, except the ones we humans create here on earth, but when the day of your happiness comes, be sure that your mother and I, wherever we are, will be smiling down on you together.

The enclosed package contains the only book left of your mother's diaries. She burned all the other volumes before she left Monksdale for the last time; this is the one she kept, writing in it only spasmodically during the last months of her life. By her wish, Jenny, I kept it to be given to you when we were both gone.

God bless you and keep you, our dear little daughter.

Charles

10th July, 1863

Margaret's wedding day, and she was every inch the White Rose as she walked down the church aisle in her lace gown; so virginal in her Grandmother Rosellen's flowing veil, her skirt and petticoats caught up with knots of rosebuds over a bell-shaped hoop.

Mr. Nesbit seems kind and devoted to her; I pray he may continue to be and that their love endures. If he is not an intelligent man, it matters not, for in all honesty, though I love her dearly, intelligence would be wasted on Margaret.

I am so grateful for the settlement that her husband made on her; it ensures that she will have money of her own to fall back on in case of need.

During the marriage ceremony, when the bridegroom promised, "With all my worldly goods, I thee endow," tears coursed down my cheeks. Fortunately, this show of emotion was mistaken for the natural sentiment of the bride's mother when what I was really weeping for was the awful irony of those words.

The bridegroom always promises to endow his wife with all his worldly goods, instead of which it is most often the other way around. The marriage settlement usually means that he receives her money, and she is left penniless and dependent, indeed becomes part of his goods and chattel.

It was my own misfortune, perhaps, that I was not brought up like the typical girl of our class and age, skilled only in acquiring a husband, not knowing household management, and unable to converse with men about politics or world events.

Had I stayed more like Margaret, innocent and ignorant, my husband might not have become impatient with me so soon. But then—God forgive me—nothing could have saved me from being unutterably bored with Sir Lewis before we were a month married!

Brighton
18th January, 1864

Nothing I ever read in a novel can approach the awesome wonder of real life.

I know now what I have suspected since before I left Monksdale—that I have not long to live, and the very man I pressed to tell me the truth, Sir Charles Melville, my specialist, is the source of the greatest happiness I have ever known.

He has changed my whole world, and I his.

Although we have both been married—he is a widower—we have neither of us known love before.

No man has been in my bed since the early months of my last pregnancy in 1845 when Sir Lewis thought that my unborn child would be a boy, not a third girl.

How I used to grit my teeth to endure his puffing, pawing, panting invasion of my privacy, thankful only that with Sir Lewis it seemed to be a very speedy business.

Lady Nancy Hurley once told me at a party—where the champagne had flowed quite freely—that she suffered her husband's attentions by closing her eyes and thinking of the queen. I had partaken fairly freely, too. "God forbid!" I cried aloud. "If thinking was contagious, that might mean nine children like her poor Majesty."

How grateful I was back in 1845 when my husband informed me, in anger and disdain, that since I was unable ever to bear him a son, he intended never to visit my bed again. This he presumed to be a punishment!

I never expressed such fervent thanks to God on any occasion as I did that night.

Sir Lewis also told me, thinking to hurt me, that he proposed to take a mistress. He had no idea that I called blessings down on her head, too, and prayed he would find the lady so diverting as never to dream of returning to me. Not even briefly between his whores. As though I did not know he had always taken mistresses when I was pregnant—which seemed to be almost always during the early years of our marriage.

Now, nearly nineteen years after my husband last came to my bed, I am a mistress myself. Now, nearly a quarter of a century after I first became a wife—which is to say, the unwilling vessel for a man's seed—I finally know what it is to be made love to!

3rd April, 1864

My health does not improve, but my bliss continues.

My Charles is stocky and gray-bearded, and I am middle-aged and far from well-looking. Both of us are nearer to our graves than to our youths, and we are excitedly, exquisitely, rapturously in love, as neither of us has ever been before. To have found it even so late gives joy and meaning to our whole lives.

I feel no shame, no guilt, no regret, except that we did not find each other sooner.

I know now why some women are bright-eyed and smiling in the morning.

I know what I have been missing all my married life.

We bring up our daughters to be wives and mothers without ever thinking of their happiness. I would rather my daughters had even such a brief period of shining joy, cherished, adored, and given such physical delight by a lover than years of stultifying boredom as proper, yielding, unloved Victorian wives!

As such a wife, I was an unprized possession and knew only misery. As Charles's mistress, I am free and independent. I know the blessing of love and the satisfaction of my senses.

13th September, 1864

I am sure that Jenny forgives me, but I cannot forgive myself. Because my own girlish infatuation for the handsome, charming Sir Lewis did not outlast the honeymoon, I was unfairly suspicious of Captain Fenton's looks and beguiling manners.

I would not see the real man underneath, and I deprived my beloved daughter not only of the chance to love and be loved but also of the opportunity to be removed forever from the sterility and injustices of her father's home.

If only, when I had the chance, instead of preaching caution, I had said to her, "Where your happiness is concerned, Jenny, look to your own heart."

My greatest grief now is that when I die I will leave her alone and unprotected. I do not worry about Margaret; she is safely wed. Nor about Catherine; Sir Lewis will care for her, and they are both armored in their own self-satisfaction. But Jenny— my sweet, sensitive Jenny. What is to become of her?

1st October, 1864

I suggested to Charles the idea that has been in my mind these many weeks. He was not even surprised. Thus do we read each other's minds.

He has agreed. When the time is right, he will ask Jenny to marry him so that he may take care of her.

He will have the few years left to him to work at her self-confidence, so eroded over the years by her father and her sad love affair.

And she will take care of him, so he will not be alone at the end but cherished even as I am.

If Jenny will not have him—and I know of only one reason she might refuse—then he will still look after her. He will protect her from her father's ill will and provide for her financially.

To know that I have found a protector for her has rid me of the only burden I could not bear.

My heart is at peace.

9th January, 1865

Jenny just returned to me my copy of Mary Wolstonecraft's *Vindication of the Rights of Women*, the book on which my father used to say, with his lopsided grin, that I cut my intellectual teeth.

"Poor Mary," Jenny said thoughtfully, "for all she was so ahead of her time, she did not conceive of our rights as God-given. This is a passionate plea for men to give our rights back to us."

Her green eyes sparkled at me with righteous indignation. "Why should men give us our rights as a gift?" my dauntless, demure-seeming daughter demanded fiercely. "By the laws of nature, if not the law of the land, they are already inherently ours."

I must admit this aspect of the situation had not occurred to me, and I lay here thinking of it, after she went to fetch my tea.

Jenny is right. Women of our class are usually infantalized, first by education—which trains them only to get husbands, not to be able to do anything about the acquisition once achieved—and then by the law.

If we inherit money and do not marry, then we may administer our own estates at twenty-one. If we wed, however, the law immediately reduces us to the cradle.

As a wife, one does not own one's own money, property, not even the clothes on one's back, certainly not the children we bear. A husband has to support us and pay our debts. That is the extent of his legal obligations. He may neglect, beat, mistreat us with impunity, even will our inherited money to someone else. He owns us, and we are seldom a possession high in his regard.

Society looks askance at mistresses, but from what I can see, a high-class courtesan frequently fares better than a wife. To be the mistress of Sir Charles Melville has certainly been a happier fate than to be wife to Sir Lewis Rosellen.

10th January, 1865

Jenny and I continued our discussion where we left off yesterday. She reminded me also that Mary Wolstonecraft did not express too much sympathy for the education and plight of women not of our class.

A sad commentary on our society, she pointed out, is that those who are bullied become bullies in turn, and the very women who should sympathize most with their unfortunate sisters are often most cold and unfeeling.

The unattached woman without money has no choice but to become a companion or, more often, a governess, living in a household where she is miserably treated by her mistress, given a salary no self-respecting housekeeper would accept, of perhaps thirty-five pounds per annum. Neglected by her superiors, scorned by her equals, insulted by her inferiors, expected to be honored by the lecherous advances of male members of the household, she lives a life of great loneliness.

7th April, 1865

I am weary, so weary.

Even my hands grow palsied now when I try to write.

Charles chided me gently when I tried to apologize that I can no longer receive him in the physical way that was once my delight.

"I do not love you for that alone," he reproached me.

When the weak, foolish tears of sickness and depression oozed out of my eyes, he relented at once.

He sat down on the bed beside me, taking both my hands, pressing his lips to each in turn.

"Oh, my love, my love," he said huskily, then went on to murmur endearments that I cannot put down even here. They are for me alone.

Charles, my beloved, how you—

Chapter Fifteen

WHEN ROBERT ISRAEL—CHOSEN AFTER INTER-
views with six other architects—and his
workmen moved into Melville House, Jenny
decided to transfer to temporary lodgings on
the Marine Parade.

It was impossible for her to study Sir
Charles's complicated notes and transpose
them into interesting, readable chapters to
the accompaniment of hammering, sawing,
galloping footsteps up and down the stairs,
shouting voices, and, not infrequently, loud
and explicit cursing.

She rode out every morning in her carriage
to confer with Mr. Israel and to satisfy herself
that all was going forward as it should.

With Miss Sayers to act as her secretary—"I
would rather earn the salary you are paying
me than sit idly around, Lady Melville"—she
devoted her afternoons to writing.

Shortly before Sir Charles's quarters were

due for renovation, Jenny steeled herself to the task of disposing of his personal effects.

It was not so difficult as she had expected.

His few bits of jewelry were already in her possession, as were all of his papers.

It was just a matter of going quickly through his clothes before they were packed away to be sent to Saint Thomas Hospital. A few odd coins, an occasional letter, or a bill long since paid came to light, but nothing more until Jenny took down the suit of mourning clothes her husband had worn the previous year when they had visited Monksdale Abbey so she could attend the funeral of the Carroll family.

Finding a letter in the jacket pocket from the law offices of Mr. Wickersham, Jenny casually opened it. Her disbelieving eyes swept across the heading.

**Private. To Sir Charles Melville.
Personal Report on David Fenton.**

Feverishly, she read on, the names dancing up and down before her on the sheet like spots before a blind man's eyes.

... *Daughter of Lord Beckwith* ... *Miss Clara Summerhouse* ... *the actress Sheila Dale* ... *Liverpool* ... *Mrs. Maxwell* ... *villa in Richmond* ... *when he goes to London* ...

Jenny crushed the paper in her hands. Such a private, personal report. Why ever had Sir Charles—

And David—

Frantically, she smoothed the single page out to read it over again. Lord Beckwith's daughter was Lady Rickles, thank God. And Miss Clara Summerhouse, who was looking elsewhere, had presumably—it was to be hoped—found someone, since it must be more than a year since the report.

Why, why had Sir Charles procured this information? For what reason? And what use had he made of it?

And why did Janet, Lady Melville, care whether David Fenton, Earl of Denby, was married or not?

His mistresses— If her mother was to be believed, and Jenny had every reason to believe her, the mistresses of men of fortune and estate frequently fared far better than their wives.

For the third time she perused Mr. Wickersham's private report.

Sheila Dale. An actress. Probably a beautiful, seductive actress. Even the name suggested allure.

Mrs. Maxwell in a villa in Richmond. She sounded cozy and domestic.

Liverpool and London. He was taken care of, obviously, on both fronts.

"No wonder he never married," said Jenny aloud in some bitterness. There was no need.

Ah, but now the situation had changed. The Earl of Denby, like Sir Lewis and all men of their like, would be seeking an heir.

Soon a suitable woman would have the privilege of receiving him into her bed—between his visits to Sheila Dale and Mrs. Maxwell—so that, in return for a comfortable life and the status of a title, she might breed him a son.

Whether this woman would be fortunate or unfortunate, Jenny could not determine.

She folded the letter up very small and tucked it inside the bosom of her gown, to be transferred later to a file of her own private papers.

Then she went on with the task of packing away Sir Charles's wardrobe.

During the weeks that followed, the report proved something of a magnet. She was drawn to the file box where it reposed as by an irresistible force, and she read it at least once a day.

Otherwise, she occupied herself sensibly with finishing the first of Sir Charles's books promised to Mr. Ellis, she worked on the outline for a book of her own, and she attended to a voluminous correspondence.

"You have not answered your sister's letter, inviting you to be godmother to her son," Miss

Sayers reminded her at their daily work session, immediately after lunch one Friday afternoon.

"Oh, dear. Well, thank her for the honor. Say I am too engaged with my work to leave Brighton just yet, and I will write a check to enclose for young Lewis." She made a moue of distaste. "Another Sir Lewis to follow after his father Sir Henry. Trust Catherine."

"The change of a visit home might do you good," suggested Miss Sayers, who knew little of the situation at Monksdale.

"Rest assured," said her employer cynically, "my sister Catherine will be much more pleased by the check than by my presence. I am certain a future bequest was in her mind when she proposed me for this honor. Any other mail to be answered today?"

"Letters of condolence are still trickling in. Shall I answer them in the usual way?"

"Yes, I suppose so," said Jenny absently, frowning over her notebook. "Who are they from?"

Miss Sayers turned over the letters lying on her desk and recited rapidly, "A Mrs. Squires in Suffolk, a Dr. Teasley from Saint Thomas Hospital, Mr. Bernard Chivers in London, and Lord David Fenton, Somersetshire."

To each name Jenny had given a quick nod and said, "the usual," until Miss Sayers reached the last name.

After a moment's dead silence, Jenny held out her hand. "I did not know Lord David had written. I should like to see his letter," she said in a deliberately colorless way that did not deceive Miss Sayers for a moment. —

She stared at Lady Melville's bowed head, speculation in her eyes.

My dear Lady Melville,

Business has taken me away from Fairburn for some time, and not until I returned and perused all my piled-up copies of the Times *did I learn the sad news of your husband's passing. Although I only met him twice, I conceived a great admiration and respect for Sir Charles.*

"Hypocrite!" thought Jenny indignantly, looking up from the note in her hand, the remembrance as fresh in her mind as though it had been the day before of the revulsion in Lord David's voice and manner when she first pointed out Sir Charles as her husband. *It is worse even than I thought. That gray-beard; why, he looks old enough to be your grandfather.*

She went on with her reading.

I hope you know that my thoughts and sympathy are all with you. Hopefully, you will visit in Somersetshire soon, and I may offer my condolences in person.

Jenny took a sheet of her elegant engraved stationery from the desk drawer and dashed off an answer to David in her own hand.

My dear Lord David,

Thank you for your message of sympathy. My dear husband's death, though not unexpected, has indeed left a void in my life. It is true that he was a man for whom no amount of respect or admiration could be too great.

Although Catherine has asked me to be godmother to her infant son, I have been forced to decline the honor, being occupied with the writing of Sir Charles's last medical texts and also the establishment of a convalescing home in his honor.

I do not, therefore, expect to have the pleasure of seeing you in Somersetshire at any time in the foreseeable future.

She passed her sealed note over to Miss Sayers for the regular post, after which they continued dealing with the mail, mostly bills, and then a letter from Margaret that set Jenny chuckling.

Miss Sayers looked at her inquiringly.

"From my other sister," explained Jenny, holding a pink, scented sheet up by one corner. "She is expecting her third child the end of the year and would like me to be godmother."

"Another check?" smiled Miss Sayers.

"With a silver christening mug," grinned Jenny, "which I shall present in person at the ceremony. Margaret asked me to be godmother to her first daughter—she has two—before ever I was Lady Melville, so I acquit her of mercenary motives."

She handed over the letter. "Please tell her—with all the proper flowery flourishes—that I will be pleased to accept, and leave the letter open so that I may add a few lines after my signature."

When this was done, Jenny stood up. "I think that finishes us for the day, Miss Sayers. Now, what I need—you may take your time about it—is two fair copies each of this book outline to be sent to Mr. Ellis, and also of these sample chapters."

Miss Sayers looked down with a puzzled frown at the papers that had been handed to her.

"*On Women and Wives*," she read aloud slowly. "Outline for a book of essays by Janet Melville.

"Why, Lady Melville, you mean this is your own *original* work?" she gasped out, awed.

"My very own original work," confirmed Jenny, laughing but pleased.

Miss Sayers studied the sample chapters.

"'The Infantilization of Wives,'" she murmured, skimming the dozen pages.

She did not read aloud again, but Jenny knew, by the way her face and neck became a study in scarlet, when she came to the second sample chapter, "On Choosing to Become a Mistress."

Chapter Sixteen

JENNY HAD JUST STEPPED OUT OF HER CAR-
riage and was mounting the steps of Melville
House when the uniformed telegraph mes-
senger rode into the driveway.

"Will you please wait? There might be an
answer."

She unfolded the sheet composedly, being
so accustomed to receiving telegraphs of business that the sight of the familiar envelope
had not caused her a moment's alarm.

With surprise greater than shock, she read,
"Sir Lewis has had serious heart seizure. Dr.
Dillon holds no hope of recovery." It was
signed Henry Rosellen.

Jenny took a pencil from her purse, scribbled an answer on the back of her own
telegraph message, and got back into her
carriage to return to the Marine Parade apartment.

Miss Sayers helped Peggy with the packing

while Jenny wrote up a list of instructions for the time she might be away. Her landlady stocked a basket of food for the journey, and, within three hours of receiving the telegraph, she was sitting in a railway car bound for Fairburn.

As the train rattled along, she was reminded uncomfortably of the last line in her letter to Lord David: "I do not expect to have the pleasure of seeing you in Somersetshire at any time in the foreseeable future."

Oh, well, she told herself, shrugging, the man of many mistresses was hardly likely to misjudge her motives. Her father's dying was certainly excuse enough for a change in plans.

A hired brougham took Jenny the last lap of her journey from the railway station to Monksdale. While Peggy supervised the coachman's unloading of her luggage, she descended from the carriage and mounted the Abbey steps, realizing the moment she saw an old-fashioned hatchment draped in oversized bows of black crape fastened to the door knocker that she had not arrived in time.

Her father was not dying; he must be dead.

Temperley, the aged butler who opened the door to her, confirmed this at once.

"Oh, Miss Jenny," he quavered, "the master's gone."

They had grown old together, Sir Lewis and his butler.

"He feels it more than I," thought Jenny compassionately, and since no one else was by, she placed a brief kiss on Temperley's cheek and pressed one gnarled hand in sympathy.

Then Catherine and her husband were with her. Catherine was in the same red-eyed, swollen-faced condition she had deplored in Lady Eleanor not so long ago. The new baronet was barely concealing his inner satisfaction under a mask of polite social grief.

"Jenny."

"Catherine."

Each accepted and bestowed a chaste embrace.

"Welcome to our home, Lady Melville," said Catherine's husband with all his usual pomposity. "It grieves me that it cannot be on a happier occasion."

Jenny inclined her head. "Thank you, Sir Henry," she said quietly and saw the ghost of a smile quickly erased from his lips.

The gleam of pleasure in his eyes remained undiminished, for which she could not fault him. He had wanted to be Sir Henry, master of Monksdale. His ambition was achieved.

Only Catherine, like Temperley, was truly bereft. She had loved her father.

"It would be nice to be able to feel sorrow,"

Jenny found herself thinking later in her old bedroom as Peggy unpacked her bags. "I would gladly trade the pain of loss for this awful lack of all feeling."

She had arrived in time for the funeral, which was held the next day. Properly gowned in a simple black taffeta dress, with rows of ruching around the neck instead of a collar, Jenny stood to the left of Sir Henry while Catherine leaned heavily on his right arm. Margaret's husband had telegraphed that she was too near her time to make the journey.

All the gentry of the county attended, of course, and Jenny spotted Lord David almost at once but would not meet his eyes, keeping her own fixed on the ugly family mausoleum, where Sir Lewis would join the rest of his illustrious ancestors in entombment instead of being buried alongside his wife.

Catherine had insisted on it, and Jenny had not demurred, glad to let her mother be apart from Sir Lewis in death as she had been in life. Lady Caroline belonged to Sir Charles Melville, and the churchyard at Brighton contained a memorial tablet to both of them, as would the Melville Convalescing Home.

When the brief ceremony was over, and Catherine, supported by her solicitous husband and followed by a trail of guests, moved toward the house, Jenny turned quietly in the opposite direction to the grave beyond the mausoleum.

She had purposely not worn a hoop so she could sit down on the grass next to the grave, which she did, quite careless of her billowing skirt and petticoats.

She scattered the sheaf of roses she had brought with her over Lady Caroline's grave.

"Your favorite flowers," she said aloud. "You will understand, won't you, if I never visit here again? I have no reason now to come to Monksdale, and it holds only bitter memories. At Brighton, Mama, you are always with me, you and Sir Charles."

She bowed her head, and the hands with which she covered her face held the rich, bittersweet scent of roses. They reminded her not only of her mother but also of the day in the Carroll garden when she had parted with David.

She felt rather than saw a shadow over the grave, dropped her hands, dashed away her tears, and said composedly, "Good morning, Lord David."

The Earl of Denby, funereal-looking in his black trousers and frock coat, hat in hand, responded, "I am very sorry for your loss, Je—Lady Melville."

Jenny lifted a rose from her mother's grave and brushed it nervously against her cheek.

"It has been several years. I've had time to grow accustomed."

"I meant—"

"Oh, my husband. Thank you, but I had your letter of condolence."

"I was referring to the loss of your father, Jenny."

Jenny carefully replaced the rose in front of the marble headstone and rose to her feet, ignoring the hand outstretched to help her.

"We need not play games, you and I, David," she said. "I have had no loss, and I will not pretend otherwise. You know as well as I that there was no love lost between my father and me. I grieved more for your aunt and uncle than I do for Sir Lewis."

"Then why were you weeping, Jenny?"

"There have been so many funerals. And in so short a time."

"I know," he agreed soberly.

"There are more people I loved dead than alive now," Jenny went on, walking toward the gates of the small cemetery. "It seems so strange."

"I am sorry," he said, following her. "Jenny, I—"

Without slackening her steps, she turned her head, a bright, artificial smile pasted on her mouth. "I must get back for the reading of the will," she told him brightly and artificially. "It will contain no surprises. Sir Henry is legal heir, and everything unentailed will go to Catherine, but protocol and my father's lawyer, Mr. MacPherson, demand that I be there."

He slipped her arm firmly through his.

"I will accompany you back to Monksdale." "Take care," he said as she stumbled; then, as she hurried on even faster than before, "I am sure MacPherson will wait for you."

"Jenny," he told her two minutes later, as she stumbled again in her haste, "I am only escorting you; I will not eat you. You may have noticed I have not even demanded conversation."

"How fortunate," said Jenny coldly, "since I have none to offer you."

"Do you still hate me, Jenny?"

She stopped short, then resumed her running walk. "Don't be absurd," Lady Melville said loftily. "I have never hated you."

"But what your hus-husband," his tongue had difficulty with the word, "said is true, isn't it? You find it hard to forgive me?"

Jenny came to a halt.

"Whenever did my husband say that to you?" she asked suspiciously.

"At Carroll House when you were paying your last visit to Nell."

"Is that when you suddenly developed such admiration and respect for Sir Charles?"

asked Jenny dryly. "I was surprised to hear you mention those feelings in your letter to me. I seem to remember quite a different response when you *spoke* of him."

"I was not in the mood to be charitable about any man you married, Jenny," he said quietly, "but I did change my mind when I had the opportunity to speak with him. He was a—an exceptional man."

"Yes, he was," Jenny agreed, "and I am glad and grateful for the years I had with him, years I would not have been granted if you had shown a little more—patience, shall we say? So, you see, David, there is nothing I have to forgive you for."

"Damn you, Jenny!" His rough hand on her arm jerked her around to confront him. "Stop giving me those sword thrusts and say what you mean."

Jenny laughed aloud, throwing back her head, letting the sound ring out, exultant and not very pleasant.

"I said *exactly* what I mean," she flung at him defiantly. "Shall I repeat it? I was never so miserable in my life as in that period when you abandoned me to unhappiness, Lord David, solely because you could not have everything your own way. After a while, however, I learned to be grateful to you. You enabled me to make my mother's last years happy. You enabled me to make Sir Charles's last years happy. Above all, your abandonment allowed *him* to make *me* happy. And now I am a rich, sought-after widow, in a very enviable position."

She wrenched her arm free of him suddenly and dipped down in a deep mocking curtsy.

"Lady Melville thanks the Earl of Denby for her fortunate lot in life, which could never have been achieved by Mrs. David Fenton."

"You bitch!" he ground out, white-faced.

Jenny said judiciously, smiling all the while, "I believe the masculine version of that epithet is bastard. I have the written evidence—as well as what I know—to prove that you, Lord David, are the very king of bastards."

Then she ran away from him, as hard as she could run; and the Earl, after his first few impulsive strides, made no attempt to follow.

He could hardly intrude on the reading of the will, but if that red-headed, rapier-tongued, unreasonable Irish Rose thought she had got the better of him, he told himself wrathfully, she had never been more mistaken.

Chapter Seventeen

ONCE THE FUNERAL WAS OVER, CATHERINE revived amazingly. Although she had been acting mistress of Monksdale Abbey for several years, to have the precious name of Lady Rosellen revived in her was a balm to her spirit that cut through the deepest grief.

As the thirteenth baronet, her husband was second in importance in the neighborhood only to the Earl of Denby. And until the earl married, she, Catherine, Lady Rosellen of Monksdale, would walk first out of every drawing room in the county and be seated in the highest position at every dinner table.

The subject of the future Countess of Denby was a topic of conversation at the Abbey far more often than it was at Carroll House.

With the same disregard that Sir Lewis had displayed for the fact that his younger daughter had once been destined to play the role of David Fenton's wife, Catherine discussed over and over the candidates to be the earl's bride.

On the fourth day of Jenny's visit, when they were still receiving visits of condolence, Catherine announced exultantly to her sister, after the last visitor departed, that she knew the name of the lucky girl.

"Mrs. Duckworth told me in confidence. Her butler had it from the Denby housekeeper. Lord David is secretly betrothed to his cousin Letitia Carroll."

Jenny's heart took a sickening plunge to the nether region of her stomach. When it came somewhat back to where it belonged and she was sure she could command her voice, she managed to say with a fair degree of calmness, "I don't recall hearing of a Carroll cousin named Letitia."

"Well, she's a twice-removed cousin. I think," said Catherine excusingly, "she was in the nursery when we were all out since she is only sixteen now."

"Sixteen!" Jenny exclaimed, then bit back the rest of what she had been about to say. To deplore such a difference in age would come strangely from a woman who had been married to a man thirty years her senior.

But that was different, argued Jenny rebelliously, with only herself to offer any dispute. Hers had not been a marriage in the ordinary sense, while David—

t be here above half the time myself, as I ve pressing business in Liverpool and Lon- n."

Jenny's hands crushed the napkin in her p while she managed to reply collectedly Sir Henry's inanities. Sheila Dale in Liver- ol. Mrs. Maxwell in London. So it was ue.

"Pressing business, indeed!" whispered atherine to Jenny, as the ladies departed the ble, leaving the gentlemen to their wine. "I ave heard that he has mistresses in both ties. And Letitia is being prepared for her le as chatelaine of Carroll House. Oh, well, e Countess of Denby, mistress of Carroll ouse, will have no cause to repine. She will ave his name and bear his sons."

"In which case," Jenny whispered back fu- ously, "it would appear to me that it is his istresses who have no cause to repine. *They* ill not be abandoned in the country or have bear his sons while he takes his pleasures the city!"

While Catherine turned to the vicar's wife, r face still registering shock at her sister's ords, Jenny, looking every inch Lady Mel- le in her Worth evening gown, swept out of e drawing room with a murmured excuse out a telegraph she had to send.

Addressed to Mr. Ellis, Sir Charles's pub- her, the message was stark and simple:

Sixteen! Why, she had been just six months short of that when first he waltzed with her. It must, she thought bitterly, be the magic age for His Lordship, the Earl of Denby.

"I wonder," she said aloud, seemingly casu- al, "that Lord David does not choose someone who is not so recently removed from the nurs- ery."

"But Jenny, she's so suitable," Catherine protested. "The only unmarried female Car- roll cousin. And Lord David is not in a hurry for his heir, though naturally he'll want one, and with Carroll blood. After all, the Fentons were nothing compared to the Carrolls. In the meantime, he can have his fun."

"His fun?" echoed Jenny stupidly.

"Oh, come now, Jenny, you're a widow—you know men—and he was a sailor, too. He's supposed to have dozens of mistresses."

In spite of the dull ache of misery that had engulfed her since Catherine first divulged her news, Jenny could not hold back a faint smile. "Several, perhaps; dozens, I doubt. He would need more time and strength than any one man could boast."

"Jenny!" exclaimed Catherine, shocked, but her husband chuckled.

"She has you there, my dear," Sir Henry said jovially.

With a murmured excuse, Jenny got up and left the room. Until it was time to dress for dinner, she lay on her bed, staring up at the ceiling with tearless eyes, furiously upbraiding herself for regarding this as a new bereavement, as though David was more lost to her because of this than he had ever been.

In a spirit of determined defiance, she put on her best black evening dress, the one Sir Charles had ordered for her from Worth shortly after their marriage. The billowing skirt had a broad front panel of cut velvet motifs. Its bell-shaped sleeves and neck trim were entirely of Chantilly lace, ornamented with black velvet bows. Elbow-length gloves of French kid, a beaded bag from Paris, and a dainty black lace fan completed her outfit.

With her foxfire hair pulled back from the perfect oval of her face and piled high in a swirled chignon, face powdered, lips slightly rouged, she was elegance personified, as far removed from little Jenny Rosellen as the dashing widowed Lady Melville could make herself.

"By Jove!" was all Sir Henry could say when he saw her, while Catherine, the Dark Rose, lovely-looking but a bit dowdy in her old black moire, could only stare in mixed surprise and envy.

As she accepted a glass of wine from her admiring brother-in-law and saw that there were unexpected guests for dinner, Jenny was doubly glad of her appearance. Her gladness

trebled when the last arrival prove[d] Earl of Denby.

Jenny was partnered by her brot[her] for dinner, while Catherine bagged Listening with one ear to Sir Henry'[s] compliments, interspersed with si[ghs] tails of the last days of Sir Lewis, Je[nny] able to absorb more than a smatterin[g] sister's conversation with Lord David

At one point she distinctly heard h[er] "My cousins, Mr. and Mrs. Harold [ ] will be visiting me soon with their dau[ghter]

Jenny, smiling sweetly at Sir Hen[ry] enormous gratitude to Catherine for [ ] abashed curiosity.

"Would that be little Letitia Carroll[ ] heard her sister ask.

"Yes, a charming girl. Have you met Lord David asked.

Catherine laughed affectedly, her s[ ] cant glance inviting Jenny's agreemen[t] the situation.

"Oh, yes, years ago, when she was j[ust a] freckle-faced child. But I gather she is pretty now?"

"Very pretty," said David, "and a grown-up."

"Will their visit be a long one?"

"I hardly know. Their own home is [being] renovated, so I have put Carroll Hou[se at] their disposal for as long as they need.

Request title change for my book, as follows: *On Women, Wives, and Whores.*"

Half an hour after Temperley had been charged with sending off her telegraph, Sir Henry, Lord David, and the other male guests entered the drawing room.

Jenny was standing at the window, holding the crimson velvet draperies to one side so she could look out at a star-studded sky. She was unconscious of the beautiful and dramatic figure she presented, black against scarlet, slender white arms upraised and full, rounded breasts straining upward from her décolletage.

Sir Henry noticed and tugged at his black cravat, momentarily forgetting that he had an urgent matter to discuss with his sister-in-law. The vicar decided innocently that little Jenny had grown into a remarkably beautiful woman. Mr. Murdoch looked from Lady Melville to his horse-faced wife and experienced sudden revulsion. Lord David Fenton, Earl of Denby, swore softly under his breath, grateful that the fullness and length of his cutaway coat preserved him from making a most embarrassing spectacle of himself.

The scene dissolved. Aware of stabbing eyes at her back, Jenny turned and dropped both her arms and the curtains, permitting her bosom to settle modestly back into the confines of her gown. The gentlemen dispersed about the room, and Lord David strode purposefully toward Lady Melville, who lifted her chin and stood her ground, as though daring him to try to intimidate her.

He came close, unconsciously sniffing at the sweet lavender scent of her perfume. In a voice of husky intimacy, he said to her, "You have come a long way in your Parisian gown, Lady Melville, from the plump little dumpling in white muslin petticoats and pink-ribboned pantaloons."

Jenny blushed slightly in mixed pleasure and confusion, but before she could answer was accosted by her host.

"My dear Lady Melville," said Sir Henry, "there appears to be some error. The telegraph you requested Temperley send out in the morning . . ."

He paused, and Jenny said coolly, "Yes, what about it, Sir Henry?"

"The message must have been written down wrong, my dear sister. I feel sure that you—" He paused delicately. "It could not possibly be—"

"If I might see it," said Jenny and, without leave, she snatched at the paper he was holding in his hands.

"This is my writing," she said coldly after a ten-second perusal. "The message seems perfectly plain to me."

"My dear Jenny!"

"My dear Henry! Why is it difficult to comprehend what is written here? It is addressed to my publisher," she said, not so much for Sir Henry's benefit as for Lord David's.

Again, for the earl's discomfiture, she read aloud:

"Request title change for my book, as follows: *On Women, Wives, and Whores.*"

"Jenny!" said the scandalized baronet, dropping his monocle while his face took on a rich ruby glow.

Lord David snorted in a most ungenteel style, and when Jenny looked sweetly, smilingly over at him, she saw that he was quite red-faced, too, not in embarrassment like Sir Henry but with suppressed laughter.

"Do you know so much about the subject, Jenny?" he asked her.

"Why should I not?" asked Jenny. "I have played all three roles."

With the words she had the painful satisfaction of seeing all the color leave his face while they exchanged glare for glare, her eyes boldly defiant, his blazingly angry.

Chapter Eighteen

ORIGINALLY, JENNY HAD PLANNED TO LEAVE the Abbey as soon as she decently could. A week's visit following Sir Lewis's funeral had seemed proper enough and as much penance as she need pay before she could return to Brighton.

Peggy had already started to pack her bags when her mistress decided—hating herself for the weakness—to delay her departure until the formerly freckle-faced but now supposedly pretty and charming Letitia came to visit Carroll House.

The girl, now gossiped about all over the county as the earl's prospective bride, arrived only two days after the dinner at Monksdale, and Sir Henry and Lady Rosellen, together with Lady Melville, were bidden to meet her at luncheon on the following afternoon.

Out of respect for their mourning state, it

would be just a quiet family affair, the earl specified in his note of invitation.

Catherine, much gratified by the attention as well as the opportunity to be first with any choice morsel of gossip concerning the first citizen of Fairburn, accepted at once. She did so without reference to either of the other two invited guests, both of whom—though for far different reasons—were more than willing.

Jenny, feeling the need for all the added confidence she could muster, lightened her mourning dress of shimmering black silk with an elaborate white chiffon Alençon lace fichu.

Little Letitia Carroll, she was pleased to note on meeting, though sweetly pretty in her pale pink muslin, with brown, sausage-like curls dancing around a moon-shaped face that still bore the mark of freckles, could hardly compare in looks to the elegant Lady Melville.

The elegant Lady Melville, however, could not hang onto the Earl of Denby's arms as Letitia Carroll most definitely did, positively hugging him and looking up at him with eyes of canine adoration; hanging, too, on each word that fell from his lips as though it were a precious gem.

The earl, Jenny thought, responded to Letitia rather as though she were a favored dog, patting her head occasionally and subduing her wildest bursts of enthusiasm with just a smile or a frown. Jenny almost expected him to feed her a tidbit from the table.

Oh dear, she thought in mixed remorse and ruefulness, did I look and act like that in the old days?

It was obvious that the earl was not in love with his distant cousin and just as plainly apparent that the Carrolls were intent on promoting a marriage.

Suitable, Catherine had said. A most suitable match. The poor, dull little girl could stay on in Somersetshire and bear his children while he philandered with his mistresses in London and Liverpool.

"I would philander him!" muttered Jenny under her breath, glowering so fiercely across the luncheon table at her host and his clinging cousin that both were considerably startled.

David stared back at her, his eyes full of speculation, shifting—as though he had just read her mind—to genuine amusement.

Flushing, Jenny lowered her head and concentrated on her fish. After a silence that lasted until the meat course, she recalled her company duty and engaged in conversation with her luncheon partner, the corpulent Mr. Carroll.

It was not too taxing an exercise since he far preferred eating to talk. While Jenny merely pushed the food about on her plate and discussed the beauties of Brighton, Mr. Carroll devoured huge quantities of beef, green vegetables, and potatoes, washing the portions down his throat with glass after glass of wine.

Presented with a trifle, some fruit, and cheese for dessert, he belched in genuine astonishment, "Bless my soul! No apple pie?"

The earl prepared to send a message of inquiry to the kitchen until Mrs. Carroll shook her head in disapproval at her husband.

Yielding to this unspoken marital message, he promptly urged his host, "No, no, my dear fellow, don't bother. I assure you, this will do very well." He cast a disparaging glance at the hanging baskets of assorted fruits and the plate of trifle before him.

Jenny gurgled into her own glass of wine, Catherine placed a napkin to her lips to hide a smile, and Letitia, with the bumbling gaucherie of youth, told her parent forthrightly, "You don't need apple pie, Papa. You are fat enough already."

The earl, his own lips twitching perilously, told Letitia with a yank at one sausage curl, "Mind your tongue, young lady. You are not too old to send back to the nursery."

Letitia subsided, blushing furiously, while Mrs. Carroll looked torn between strangling either her husband or her daughter.

Mr. Carroll, having disposed of a peach and

a cluster of grapes, began trifling with his trifle and made dutiful conversation with Jenny. "And when do you return to Brighton, ma'am?" he asked her.

"Tomorrow morning," returned Jenny promptly, having just that moment reached the decision.

"Tomorrow!" The word seemed to be echoed around the table, Catherine and Sir Henry both uttering it in accents of surprise and the earl with a good deal of displeasure.

"I had no idea you were leaving so soon, Lady Melville," Lord David addressed her across the table.

"My stay here has already been longer than I intended," she murmured. "I have work to do in Brighton regarding my convalescing home." She stared challengingly across at him. "And my books. In addition, I may have to spend some time in London, too, on other business."

There were compensations for growing older, Jenny reflected a little later, as she thanked the Earl of Denby for luncheon and bade him good-bye. One was less likely to wear one's heart on one's sleeve.

Little Jenny Rosellen, feeling as she did now, would no doubt have wept or blushed or looked into Lord David's face with a similar doglike devotion to that shown by his sixteen-year-old cousin.

Lady Melville did none of these things. Lady Melville had pride and poise and polished company manners. She could make her last farewells as though the Earl of Denby was nothing to her and it hardly mattered that they might never meet again.

A telegraph and a letter awaited Jenny's return to Monksdale.

The telegraph from Mr. Ellis agreed to the title change she had suggested and requested that she expand the chapter "On Choosing to Become a Mistress."

The letter from Mr. Wickersham mentioned that he planned to attend the Irish Rose shareholders' meeting in Liverpool the following week, carrying on for her as usual, unless he received contrary instructions.

Jenny carried both telegraph and letter up to her bedroom and handed them to Peggy.

"Please put these in my portfolio," she said wearily. "I'll need to draft answers when we get home."

She reached behind her to unbutton the black silk dress, and Peggy came to help her. Between them they disposed of most of her petticoats and her hoop. Then she changed into a simple black and white cotton that she wore at home in Brighton when no visitors were expected or admitted.

"If Lady Rosellen should inquire, I have

gone for a short stroll," she told Peggy, inserting her feet into a pair of stout walking shoes.

Seeing the maid's look of dismay at the shoes and the old black shawl she snatched up on her way to the door, she told her, "Don't worry, Peggy. I shall use the back stairs. I'm going to say good-bye to Mama."

She met two housemaids and one footman on the back stairs and received two flustered curtsies and one awkward bob before they flattened themselves against the wall to let her pass. Once safely in the kitchen garden, she met no one until she reached the small cemetery and passed by the mausoleum.

Lord David Fenton, Earl of Denby, hatless and still dressed in the light waistcoat and narrow-collared jacket he had worn to luncheon, rose from her mother's grave, brushing off the seat of his brown tweed trousers. He looked very matter-of-fact and master of the situation.

"I felt sure if you were leaving tomorrow morning you would probably be here some time today."

"But what on earth—" Jenny began and was ruthlessly interrupted.

"I knew if I waited long enough you would come."

"But why?"

"I should think that was obvious," said Lord

David almost disdainfully. "I want you to marry me, Jenny."

"*Marry* you!" Jenny squealed.

"Yes, marry me," David laughed. "What's so astonishing about that, Jenny? It's hardly a new idea."

"You're supposed to marry Letitia Carroll."

"I know the whole county has me marrying Letitia, to say nothing of the servants and Letitia's parents. The last one to be consulted on the matter was me, and I was very firm in refusal."

"Does Letitia know that?"

"If she doesn't, she soon will."

"And you don't care at all about the pain you will cause her?"

"Good God, Jenny, the girl is in the throes of calf love. I would have to be a very vain sort of fellow to believe it will last any longer than the usual feeling of that sort. The first handsome music master or army officer she meets will quickly displace me in her affections. Jenny, why the hell are we discussing my little cousin when I just asked you to marry me?"

"Because everyone considers her so suitable."

"Suitable. A child bride to bear me children?"

"Is that how you conceive of a wife? As someone to bear you children?"

He grinned and held out his hand. "I just did the proposing, Jenny. It's up to you to do the conceiving."

Jenny took a step backward. "That does not amuse me in the least."

"So I see. Perhaps we had better begin over."

Her head lifted haughtily. "Perhaps we had."

"The idea of marriage between us is not precisely new, you will admit," he said, arms folded across his chest. "Our circumstances—both our circumstances—have altered considerably since we first contemplated it, but I don't see that as a bar to happiness.

"You are, as you pointed out to me," he added dryly, "a rich, sought-after widow, and I am a rich, sought-after earl." His laughing eyes invited her to join in his amusement. "Frankly, I would greatly appreciate the protection marriage might bring me of not being so sought-after."

Jenny remained stonily silent.

With a shrug and a sigh, he continued, "I know you have work of your own which is important to you—your convalescing home, Sir Charles's projects—and I would do my best not to interfere with any of these. As a matter of fact, I have business interests of my own that would take me to

Liverpool and London a good deal of the time."

Jenny began breathing like a race horse in the last lap around the course. "And you would not expect me to go on these business trips with you?" she asked him, nostrils flaring.

"I said I would try not to interfere with your concerns," he repeated doggedly.

"How kind, how thoughtful!" said Jenny all on a breath. "So you would be willing to go to Liverpool and London alone and leave me—here—where?"

"The truth is," he explained patiently, "when I first came into the title, I thought of selling Carroll House. After all, it's not an old family estate. Uncle William's father bought it only forty years ago. I consulted Nell—I would not want to give her more sorrow—and she said to do as I pleased, she never wanted to come here again, it would be far too painful. The only reason I thought of holding onto Carroll House was for you, Jenny. After all, you are Somerset born and bred, and I thought—"

He knew by her unyielding face that this scene was going very badly, but he was nonetheless determined to see it through.

"I thought, a country home—to bring up our children—"

He came to a stumbling halt, made aware

by her scorching glance that he had somehow blundered again. Why on earth was she so infuriated by the notion of children?

"I did think—I did want—surely it's not unexpected to want children in a marriage?"

"*I* never had any," said Jenny.

Lord David winced. In spite of his late-grown respect and admiration for Sir Charles, to picture Jenny in his elderly embrace—

"Your husband may have been too old!" he blurted out.

"My husband was twice the man you will ever be!" Jenny hurled at him in a frantic need to hurt.

"He said you would find it hard ever to forgive me. Is that true, Jenny?"

"You are bloody right it's true, especially when you come here and insult me."

"Insult you! Damnation, girl, I asked you to marry me. Since when is that an insult?"

"Since you plan to go on with your life in Liverpool and London as before. Well, let me tell you, Lord David Fenton, Earl of Denby, I have plans of my own for how I intend to lead my life, and they definitely do not include being your stay-at-home wife."

"What plans? What do you mean, stay-at-home?"

"Go to Liverpool! Go to London!" said Jenny. "You'll find out."

"I'll find out now—this minute!" said Lord

David, advancing on her, a martial light in his eyes and a pugnacious thrust to his chin.

As he put out both hands to seize hold of her shoulders, Jenny took him by surprise with the suddenness and strength of her hand shoving at his midsection.

With a grunt of pain, he went stumbling backward, tripped over an old half-hidden headstone, and sat down hard on the ground. Before he could pull himself together, Jenny had picked up her skirts and run as hard and as fast as she could out of the cemetery, back to the safety of Monksdale.

Chapter Nineteen

JENNY'S ARRIVAL IN LIVERPOOL WAS DELIBER-
ately timed to be thirty-six hours in advance
of the shareholders' meeting. She was preceded by Mr. Wickersham, who had traveled up
from London one day earlier.

A note next to the flowers in her hotel suite
informed her that the attorney would meet
her at six in the lady's writing room so
they could dine early before going on to the
theater.

"I have been so fortunate," the note con-
cluded in his small neat script, "per your
instructions, as to obtain a box for a revue
featuring the actress Miss Sheila Dale."

Later that evening, wearing her black satin
Worth gown, Jenny sat in the box he had
obtained, her glasses trained on the stage
where Miss Sheila Dale pirouetted and co-
quetted with her audience, singing popular
ballads of the day in a throaty, seductive voice

and allowing tantalizing glimpses of her ankles each time she flipped up her skirts.

"Dear me," said Mr. Wickersham, surprised at all the cheering. "She does not seem very talented."

"She does not need to be," said Jenny cynically, laying the glasses on the empty seat behind her. Then she frowned a little, wrinkling her nose and her forehead. "She reminds me of someone," she mentioned, puzzled. "I can't think who."

"Why, I believe yourself, my dear Lady Melville," Mr. Wickersham told her, then added hastily, "A much cruder version, that is to say. She is not, of course," he pointed out with snobbish simplicity, "a lady. But the reddish hair, the facial coloring and contours—why, even the figure—"

His voice trailed away into nothingness under the concentrated outrage on Jenny's similarly contoured face.

"You're right, you're absolutely right!" she gasped, and the attorney's breathing eased.

For a bad moment he had interpreted her expression to mean that she was mortally offended by such a comparison, whereas Jenny's fury was all directed at Lord David. How dare he choose a mistress who looked like her!

Later that night, much against his better judgment, Mr. Wickersham accompanied Jenny to the small supper club where he had learned it was Lord David's custom when in town to bring Miss Dale after her performance.

A meeting between them all was not only likely but inevitable, and it was very much on Jenny's mind when it took place that Miss Sheila Dale's lover had made do with a poor imitation when he could have had the original.

She and Mr. Wickersham were already seated when Lord David and the actress walked past on the way to their own table.

"How do you do, Lord David?" Jenny greeted him in a loud, clear voice, and he stopped so suddenly that his companion was nearly jerked free of her hold on his arm.

"Jenny!" Lord David gasped, not only surprised to see her but astonished that, contrary to custom, she would in any way acknowledge his acquaintance when he was in the company of his mistress.

Then he saw the lawyer, familiar from all the Irish Rose shareholders' meetings. "Mr. Wickersham!"

Mr. Wickersham said, "How d'you do, Lord David?" and harumphed loudly into his handkerchief. Jenny smiled sweetly up at Lord David and Miss Sheila Dale.

Awkward introductions were made all around.

"Won't you join us?" asked Jenny, all wide-eyed innocence. And the actress smiled a great wide smile and began, "Why, I don't mind if—"

She broke off, taking a little hop in the air, and Jenny, who had seen Lord David surreptitiously pinch her shoulder, dissolved into laughter as soon as they made their excuses and departed.

Mr. Wickersham removed his spectacles and polished them in great agitation.

"My dear Lady Melville," he twittered, "I wish I knew what you were about."

"Don't worry, you will," she promised, still rocking with mirth. "I think we can leave now. I did what I came to do."

In a hired brougham on the way to her hotel, Mr. Wickersham asked her with some diffidence, "Would it be impertinent, my dear, as one who has your best interests at heart, to inquire just what it was you came to that club to do?"

Jenny took his arm impulsively. "You could never be impertinent," she assured him warmly, "and in time you will know all there is to know, just as Lord David will learn tomorrow who owns the second largest block of stock in Irish Rose. For the present, though, can you not accept that I merely meant to give Lord David a rather bad night tonight—when his head should be clear—before I give him a startling surprise tomorrow?"

If Mr. Wickersham was dissatisfied, he was too much a gentleman to say so, and Lord David's name was not mentioned again between them until they took their places in a front row of chairs at the shareholders' meeting in the Merseyside Irish Rose board room the next morning.

"Is Lord David here?" asked Jenny, craning her neck toward the back of the room.

"He just stepped onto the platform," whispered Mr. Wickersham.

Jenny's eyes turned frontward toward the knot of men who quickly absorbed Lord David into their center. The group was soon involved in an animated discussion while more men continued to pour through the open doors, many of them pausing for a long, curious look at Jenny before they took their seats.

The rows of chairs were three-quarters full when Lord David finally turned around, and his eye, too, immediately lighted on her.

"Jenny!"

He spoke her name so loudly that the buzz of many conversations ceased and the room fell almost silent.

Lord David came to the edge of the platform directly in front of her, staring first at her and then at Mr. Wickersham.

"Jenny!" he said again, as though confirming his first incredulous suspicion.

He knelt swiftly, bracing one hand against the wooden platform to help him vault safely down onto the floor.

"You can't be—I stayed up all night—the two of you together—too much of a coincidence—"

She had never seen him more discomposed. It was an effect she had striven for, yet all at once she was hesitant. It was Mr. Wickersham who finally took firm, competent hold of the reins.

"I have the honor to represent Lady Melville in her financial dealings, Your Lordship," he told the Earl of Denby matter-of-factly. "Hitherto she has chosen to remain anonymous, which is why I have been her delegate at previous Irish Rose board meetings. As of now, she wishes to be acknowledged as the owner of the stock, with all voting rights and privileges vested in her rather than myself."

Lord David acknowledged this bit of business information with a curt nod and an impatient wave of one hand. His mind was moving in other channels.

"It was you," he said slowly. "When the line was in danger of being sunk, *you* started buying, *you* reversed the trend, *you* saved Irish Rose."

His eyes darted for a moment from her to Mr. Wickersham. "Or were you advised—?"

"Lady Melville," Mr. Wickersham said swiftly before his client could speak for herself, "acted on her own; that is to say, she acted *against* the advice of her then counsel."

"So it *was* you who saved me?" Lord David repeated, his eyes vibrantly alive and challenging. "At a time," he added softly, "when you had little reason to give me aid."

Jenny's brows lifted a bare fraction of an inch. There was a faint smile on her lips, but she said nothing.

Lord David stepped so near to her that she felt the pressure of his legs against her knees and blinked momentarily against the blinding brilliance of his eyes.

"Why, Jenny?" he whispered. "Tell me why."

Still Jenny did not speak, and as he reached for her hand two gentlemen dressed almost identically in suiting of a dreary snuff brown came along the aisle to catch Lord David's attention.

"Milord," murmured one, "it is past time we started."

"Lord David," said the second man, "Sir Harry Graham is waiting for you at the podium."

Lord David bent down, and in one fluid

movement caught hold of Jenny's wrist and hauled her to her feet.

"Tell Sir Harry to proceed with the meeting," he instructed crisply. "Make sure Mr. Clarence Wickersham is introduced early on," he told the first brown suit. "I shall return in no more than twenty minutes," he informed the second.

Jenny, pulled ruthlessly along the aisle that was opened up by a pair after pair of pulled-back, trousered legs, made only one stab at freedom, an attempt that was acknowledged with a contemptuous snort of laughter as the steel fingers handcuffed her wrist ever more tightly.

"Forget it, Jenny," advised David Fenton, Earl of Denby, kicking open a door and jerking her along an ill-lit hallway. "Our talk is long overdue, and I am not letting you out of my sight till we have it."

Quite content to be carried along in his wake, Jenny nevertheless could not resist a scornful little titter.

"Do you really think twenty minutes could encompass all that we have to say to each other?" she asked spitefully.

"No." He kicked open another door, pushed her into a small and rather dirty office, let go of her wrist, and slammed the door shut again. "But it will be a start."

He pointed toward a large desk chair. "Sit down."

"Thank you. I prefer to remain standing."

Lord David heaved a deep, deliberately exaggerated sigh, took her by both shoulders, and shoved her unceremoniously into the chair. "Stay seated," he said quietly enough, but Jenny, who had been about to rise up indignantly, decided that, after all, she was quite comfortable.

Lord David, who had not spent eight years in Her Majesty's navy without some experience in subduing hotblooded youngsters, permitted himself a slight, grim smile and sat opposite her on a corner edge of the battered desk that half filled the room.

"Start talking."

"About what?"

"Jenny!" he said warningly.

Jenny shrugged. "It's quite uncomplicated," she said matter-of-factly. "Sir Charles made over a great deal of money and property to me even before he died. He taught me how to manage and invest, set me up with advisors, and then allowed me to handle my investments as I saw fit."

"And just coincidentally you bought Irish Rose?"

"As a matter of fact, it was brought to my attention by my former man of affairs. He had Irish Rose in mind for long-term investment, but when you got into trouble and the *Sweet Jenny* was in jeopardy, he advised me quite strongly against the company."

"Which is when you proceeded to buy?"

"Precisely," said Jenny at her most businesslike. "The stock had fallen to its very bottom. I was able to buy up huge blocks dirt cheap."

"You knew that you risked your entire investment?"

"I knew what all the panicked sellers did *not* know," said Jenny, tight-lipped, "that you would surely recover your lost ship."

"How did you know that, Sweet Jenny?" he asked, leaning toward her.

Jenny ignored this tender play on words.

"I knew—they did not—your ambition, your grim tenacity, your ruthlessness, and your determination to show my father—and me—that you were capable of rising on your own. You needed nothing we had to offer."

"I am willing to admit all that, Jenny. Are you willing to admit the truth, too?"

"What truth would that be?"

"You had the chance to get even with me—to flatten me—to sink me for all time. Instead you chose to save my company—to save me."

"I made myself a rich woman in my own right even before my husband died."

"You could have chosen other paths to riches."

"Why should I want to be even with you?"

"Like a spoiled child in a tantrum because he couldn't have what he wanted there and then, I left you when you needed me."

"So you did," said Jenny, lips smiling, green eyes chilled, "which turned out to be the best thing that ever happened to me. I went to Brighton with my mother, and after she died I married Sir Charles."

"So you bought up my stock and saved the Irish Rose line out of gratitude?" asked Lord David ironically.

"I bought it because, among other things, I have become a very astute business woman." She laughed merrily. "Why should the reason your line was saved matter, Lord David? The fact that it *was* saved has made you a rich, important man."

"I would trade all the importance and half the riches to be able to believe that you saved me out of—out of—"

Jenny did not trouble to conceal her amusement. "Out of what, Lord David?"

"Out of—" He hesitated, mouth dry, feeling that the advantage had suddenly been swept away from him. "Out of some—some feeling you have—remaining for me."

"You mean love?" asked Jenny, laughing

out loud, making it quite evident that her laughter was directed at him.

"Yes, damn you, I mean love," said Lord David gratingly.

Then, just as he had in the board room, he seized her wrist and hauled her up, this time into his arms.

Chapter Twenty

A FEW PAPERS AND ORNAMENTS HAD BEEN swept to the floor, and, heedless of its hardness, they were lying on the desk, mouth to mouth, breast to breast, his arm beneath her neck for pillowing.

His lips moved against hers, murmuring her name alone, then coupling it with endearments—"Jenny, Jenny, sweet, adorable Jenny"—next passionately kissing her as though he would absorb into himself not only her mouth but all of her breath and her being.

His free arm went about her as his kisses deepened and drew her from passive acceptance to positive response. One-handed, he untied the strings of her bonnet and tossed it over the paperweight on the floor. He stroked her hair and her shoulders and then the rigid area at the back of her neck. His fingers slid in and around her ears and over her cheekbones, outlined her brows, and curled up her lashes, lastly pushing her chin up to further aid his devouring mouth.

Then the fingers moved down the gulping column of her throat, unbuttoning the top half-dozen buttons so his hand could slide inside her bodice.

Jenny shuddered, pushing her breasts toward the groping hand, and Lord David suddenly shuddered, too.

"Oh God, Jenny, how I want you!" she heard him utter, and she pulled a little back from him, body arched proudly, her eyes glinting with satisfaction. She had made him say it!

"So have me," invited Jenny. "I'm not—you may have perceived—struggling very hard."

She watched the blank look of amazement descend on Lord David's face. Less versed in the ways of men than she supposed, she was unaware that her words had—for the moment —also extinguished passion.

Seconds before Lord David had been fearful he would disgrace himself badly by his body's inability to wait on their coupling. Now all amorous feelings were quenched as he pulled away to glare down at her.

How dare she refuse his honorable offer of marriage and then abandon herself this way in a dusty office—on a desk, for God's sake— like a common barmaid, eager to have her petticoats turned up and her drawers pulled down for a brief, lusty set-to?

"Are you out of your mind?" he demanded, sitting up and forcing her to sit up, too. "Or," he added almost hopefully, "don't you understand what was about to happen?"

"I thought I was about to be seduced," said Jenny coolly, looking with amusement into his furious eyes.

"And that doesn't bother you?" he shouted.

"I happen to be a widow," Jenny pointed out, primming her mouth mockingly. "We widows have greater—er—license—than unmarried maidens; almost the same freedom, mightn't one say, as mistresses?" She looked up at him questioningly.

"No, I would not say that! Widowed or not, you're a respectable woman, damn it! Not a—a slut to be—to be taken on a desk!"

"Five minutes ago," said Jenny, shouting in turn, "you were trying to take this respectable widow on that very desk."

"I know I was, and I'm ashamed of it, and you should be ashamed, too."

"Ashamed of what? Accepting your advances or not being a hypocrite and pretending they were unwelcome?"

"God damn it, Jenny!" He pounded the objectionable piece of furniture with his fist, then winced in pain. "I want to *marry* you. I want things right and proper between us."

Jenny leaned over the side of the desk,

recovering her bonnet and her temper together.

"Oh, stuff it," she said sweetly. "What you don't understand, Lord David, is that I am no longer the proper kind of person you evidently envisage as your countess and breeder of little earls. Perhaps we had better get back to the shareholders' meeting."

Lord David, who had forgotten the meeting completely, groaned out loud, yanked his round gold watch from his waistcoat pocket, and uttered a few picturesque words of profanity.

"We must get back to the meeting," he agreed savagely, "but don't let that fool you into thinking that *this* meeting between us is over. If I have to spend the rest of the day in your hotel sitting room, with Mr. Wickersham as chaperone, you and I are going to come to an understanding."

He set the papers and ornaments back on the desk while Jenny shook out her skirts and put on her bonnet. When he held the door of the grubby little office open, she moved toward it, smiling and serene.

"Your dress is unbuttoned," Lord David growled, his hungry gaze on her gaping bodice.

"To be sure it is," said Jenny, setting down her purse, her fingers deft, her expression calmly amused as she buttoned the half-dozen little pearl buttons and then preceded him through the door.

A few minutes later she was acknowledging the waves of applause that greeted her introduction by one of the men in the snuff-brown suits as the "previously unknown owner" for whom Mr. Wickersham had acted as attorney-in-fact. "Lady Janet Melville, who has done more than anyone, except Lord David Fenton himself, both to save and then reestablish the Irish Rose line as a potent force in the shipping world."

Jenny bowed, smiled, and then resumed her seat, determinedly engaging Mr. Wickersham in conversation so as to divert attention away from herself.

For the next quarter-hour, while her mind drifted far from the business at hand, she studiously avoided even a casual peek at the platform. When she finally did glance in the direction of the Irish Rose officers, David's eyes were on her, bright, fixed, and unblinking. Jenny pressed a handkerchief to her lips, holding back slightly hysterical laughter. She could swear he looked torn by agonizing regret for his lost opportunity on the battered old desk.

Well, so far as her body's yearnings were concerned, she was torn by the same regrets, but otherwise it was just as well. It had formed no part of her plans, she reminded herself briskly, to have lain with him for the first time in a grubby office overlooking the Mersey River.

Let him come to her in London, where her bedsheets were of the finest, softest old linen and her bed hangings of crushed velvet, and the noble president of the Irish Rose was no more important than Lady Melville, the writer, the rich widow of a baronet—or, at least, not too much more so!

Let him come to her in London where Sheila Dale did not cavort about the stage, exhibiting all of her ankles and half her bosom, and was obviously a far better seducer than Sweet Jenny of Brighton!

"Mr. Wickersham." She bent across to him. "Is the important business over with? May we go now?"

"Whenever you wish, my dear Lady Melville. Are you weary?"

"I want to get back to London as quickly as possible."

He looked a little puzzled but rose when she did, took her arm, and courteously led her to the double doors at the back of the board room.

One of the men in the snuff-brown trousers and jackets came panting after them as they hurried down the outside steps of the Irish Rose building.

He addressed himself to Jenny. "Lord David wishes to know where and when he may call on you."

Jenny smiled demurely, her eyes warning Mr. Wickersham against speaking, as she took a London calling card out of her purse.

With a little silver pencil, she scribbled on the back of the card, then handed it over to Lord David's man.

"I have written down the name of my hotel," she told him graciously. "Will you tell Lord David any time after tea will suit me admirably?"

"And so it will," she chuckled to Mr. Wickersham as they walked away arm in arm. "By the time he comes to the hotel seeking me, we should be on our way to London."

Mr. Wickersham could only shake his head.

Over the years he had seen dear Sir Charles's wife in many guises, many moods, and through many crises, but never before had she seemed so volatile, so unpredictable, so—

In his opinion, her ladyship was sadly underestimating Lord David Fenton, Earl of Denby. The naval officer who had started the Irish Rose line with a few thousand pounds and the purchase of one small schooner, the determined owner who had crossed an ocean and a continent to recover a lost ship and punish the thief, was not going to be so easily put upon by a slip of a girl with laughter on her lips and, obviously, a good deal of anger stored up in her heart.

Dear Lady Melville, he hoped she knew what she was doing. Despite his doubts—he squared his shoulders and started consulting a railway timetable—his job was to help her in any way he could. Whether she was right or wrong, he was her man of affairs.

The note that awaited the Earl of Denby when he arrived at Lady Melville's hotel just past tea time was deliberately precise—and provocative.

The desk clerk handed it over with the information that Lady Melville and her attorney had departed the hotel some two hours earlier.

Lord David ripped open the envelope so fiercely that the single page it contained was torn in half. He had to hold the two pieces together to read the bold slash of her scant half-dozen lines.

My dear Lord David,

Pressing business has called me to London sooner than I expected. I plan to

*remain there for three to four weeks, so
you may contact me, in case of need,
through Mr. Wickersham.*

*Yours sincerely,
Janet, Lady Melville*

Lord David crushed the two pieces of the
note between his fingers in a way that suggested that Jenny—had she been there—
might have suffered the same fate.

After this first physical outlet for his temper, he spent a satisfactory sixty seconds uttering low-voiced naval obscenities destined
to vastly enlarge the vocabulary of the sharp-
eared clerk.

Pressing business of his own, Lord David
estimated, would keep him in Liverpool another two, perhaps even three days. After
that—

If Mr. Wickersham had been present to ob-
serve the thrust of Lord David's chin, the
tightening of his lips, the cold look of calcula-
tion in his eyes, and the ominously slanting
lift of his brows, he might have said aloud to
Jenny what he had only permitted himself to
think before.

Dear Lady Melville had sadly underestimat-
ed the Earl of Denby.

Chapter Twenty-one

THEY ARRIVED IN LONDON IN TIME FOR JENNY to be cosseted by the housekeeper at Melville House with a supper tray in her bedroom and a hot bath before she retired for a sound night's sleep. She was up at her usual hour of seven, restless and unable to work.

At home in Brighton, she would have gone for a long walk along the beach before breakfast, then put in some time at her writing. This day she forced herself to wait impatiently for the hours to pass, knowing she could not in all decency pay her intended call much before the hour of eleven.

A hired carriage and coachman, arranged for by Mr. Wickersham, conveyed her to Mrs. Maxwell's villa in Richmond. It was surrounded by a high stone wall; a long graveled path, lined with thick hedges, opened into a circular driveway opposite the steps leading up to the front door.

Jenny descended from the carriage and surveyed the villa for a moment before approaching the broad steps. It was an imitation Georgian house of mellowed brick and stone, half covered with ivy creepers. The lawn in front was beautifully cropped and green. Off to one side she caught a glimpse of a rose garden and far in the distance a portion of an octagonal gazebo.

My, my, thought Jenny satirically—remembering with a pang how a mere Captain Fenton had been shown the door of her father's house—Lord David does his mistresses very well!

A respectable-looking elderly parlor maid showed Jenny into a small sitting room overlooking the rose garden and carried off her calling card on a small silver salver.

Some seven or eight minutes later, another less elderly-looking woman came into the room, shutting the door firmly behind her. This one, however, was no parlor maid in apron and cap.

Her dress was of watered blue silk just a shade darker than the improbable color of her carefully curled hair. It was cut low across a massive bosom but given respectability by the foaming folds of a lace fichu. She had a plump, rosy—perhaps too rosy—face and friendly, twinkling blue eyes, and Jenny was much mistaken if the lady would ever see fifty again.

"Mrs. Maxwell?" she asked doubtfully.

"Lady Melville?" asked Mrs. Maxwell just as doubtfully, pinching Jenny's calling card between her fingers. "Have we ever —I think I would have remembered had we met?"

"You can't be Lord David's—"

Jenny broke off, covering both crimson cheeks with her gloved hands, as aghast at her own gaucherie as at the notion that David —this woman and David—

"Oh," said Mrs. Maxwell in sudden understanding, a beaming smile breaking through the powdered mask of her face, "you're a friend of Lord David. How nice of you to call. Do sit down, dearie, and let's get acquainted while we wait for Lizzie to bring us sandwiches and tea."

A slightly dazed Jenny accepted a seat on the brocade-covered arm chair urged on her by Mrs. Maxwell before her hostess plumped herself down on the nearby sofa.

"Lord David is so thoughtful," she told her guest comfortably. "I give plenty of dinner parties, you understand, but now that I no longer have to work I do get lonely during the day, being used, as you might say, to have my friends all about me, and that's a fact."

"You don't have to work any longer?" was all Jenny could think of to say.

"Oh, my, no, the minute Lord David was on his feet—and especially after he got the title—he insisted on giving me an income. He said it was only right seeing as how I'd put my savings into Irish Rose when he got it started, so here I am," she laughed cheerfully and leaned over to pat Jenny's hand, "with more money than I ever thought to have but a bit more time on my hands than I figured on either. But, there now, that's life, isn't it? We have to take the bitter with the sweet, don't we?"

Since it seemed to be a serious question, Jenny found herself weakly answering, "I suppose we do."

Oh, God! Sheila Dale she could understand, but the man who had waltzed with her at Margaret's wedding and wooed her in the Carroll rose garden, the naval officer who had walked her down forest paths away from Nell to passionately kiss and possessively handle her, even the man who had lain with her on a hard wood desk in a Mersey office—could *he*, not once or twice but for many years, have gone to bed with this fat, friendly, decent, dye-haired woman old enough to be his mother?

"Oh, God!" said Jenny aloud.

"You're looking very pale, dearie." Her hostess jumped up. "Are you feeling under the weather?"

"G-give me s-something," implored Jenny, her voice fading away. "I don't w-want to spoil your c-carpet."

With amazing promptitude and no questions asked, Mrs. Maxwell seized on a Jasper bowl of the same delicate green that now tinged Jenny's face, emptied the water and lotus buds it contained into a potted plant, and thrust the bowl high against Jenny's chest.

She was just in time.

After a wretched few minutes, during which her hostess held the bowl steady and her guest's head as well, Jenny lifted a now scarlet face to say miserably to Mrs. Maxwell, "I don't know how to apologize to you, I—"

"Then don't even try, dearie." Mrs. Maxwell indicated the bowl. "You don't need this any more?"

"No, n-no thank you," said Jenny in a strangled voice, and the bowl was wrested from her limp hands and carried to the door.

"Lizzie!" bawled Mrs. Maxwell at the top of her powerful lungs.

On the fourth call the elderly maid appeared, and the bowl was given into her keeping. A pot of good hot tea was demanded immediately, "but never mind the sandwiches, Lizzie," Jenny heard her say and could only shudder in agreement.

Seated once again in the brocade arm chair,

while her hostess beamed at her from the sofa, Jenny carefully folded away the handkerchief she had used to wipe her mouth and once more attempted an apology.

"You mustn't take on so, dearie," Mrs. Maxwell admonished her kindly. "We're all human and have to make our mistakes. I had my turn at not knowing when enough champagne was enough. There now, let's forget about it. Something's bothering me, and that's a fact. It occurred to me, dearie—by the way, what *is* your name?"

Jenny blinked bewilderedly. "It's on my card," she said.

Mrs. Maxwell laughed so hard a dimple appeared in her quivering layer of chins. "I mean your real name, not your professional one, though I must say it sounds real elegant. Janet, Lady Melville," she recited, as though reading it, "good enough for the stage, it is."

"But that *is* my real name," protested poor Jenny, feeling as though she had wandered into a madhouse. "Janet Melville."

"You mean to say, dear—that is, you're a *real* ladyship the same as Davey is a lordship?"

"Davey," Jenny echoed, utterly bemused. Mrs. Maxwell called the formidable Earl of Denby Davey!

She found herself licking away two salt

tears that had finished a slow crawl down her cheeks. "I'm a real ladyship," she choked out. "Are you a real—a real—"

Jenny stopped in the middle of her question, as scarlet now with mortification as before she had been pale with fright. How, when she began, could she have failed to consider the insult she was offering to this woman who, whatever her position in society—or lack of it—had offered her nothing but kindness and courtesy?

Much more than courtesy, she reminded herself, benumbed. What other so-called lady of her acquaintance would have dealt so quickly and competently with a stranger's sudden illness in her drawing room, making such a minimum of fuss about the incident to spare the hapless victim embarrassment?

Resolved to begin over and do better, Jenny sat stiffly upright, unaware that her finger-nails scratching nervously at the brocade chair arms were giving her house-proud hostess a new distress.

"It's true, I am a friend of Lord David's," she made her fresh start. "His uncle—the Earl of Denby before him—was a neighbor to my family in the country. That was before I married and moved to Brighton," she hurried on. "Of course, during those years, I didn't see Davey—David—Lord Denby very often. He was abroad or in Liverpool, and I hardly ever left Brighton, so—"

"So that accounts for why he never mentioned you to me," Mrs. Maxwell cut in cheerfully, hoping to help her guest's halting story along. "With a husband in the picture, no doubt he—"

"Oh, he's dead," Jenny blurted out with all the awkward impetuosity of the girl half past fifteen who had first met Lieutenant Fenton on the stairway of Carroll House.

Blushing madly again at her own gaucherie, she stopped ripping at the brocade of the chair and instead started savaging the strings of her purse as she made a new beginning.

"Sir Charles, my dear husband, died early in the year," she explained quietly to Mrs. Maxwell. "I've been living rather retired ever since."

"Of course you have," her hostess told her comfortingly. "A real lady like yourself would be bound to. Still," she went on practically, "you can't grieve forever, especially a pretty young thing like you. You've got long years ahead of you," she added sagely, "and you have to remember that life is for the living."

Since Jenny only answered with a sound halfway between a snort and a groan, her hostess plunged on doggedly.

"I'm sure that Davey sees it the same way I

do. No doubt," she hinted, "it's why he sent you to me."

"He didn't exactly send me, not as his friend," wailed Jenny. "I came—on my own."

"Oh, my dearie, I just suddenly realized. This wasn't just a social call, was it?"

Jenny nodded dumbly.

"Lord David thought I could advise you about a new protector, that's it, isn't it?"

"Oh, good God!" said Jenny, turning slightly green again.

Mrs. Maxwell looked about in quick alarm, searching for another large receptacle. "Are you going to be sick again, dea—Lady Melville?"

"No, no, I'm fine. I just—I thought—I wanted—" Jenny had never been more tongue-tied in her life.

Mrs. Maxwell regarded her shrewdly.

"I think we've been talking at crosspurposes, and I've always been one who liked plain speaking. You came to me for a reason, my lady. Why don't you just spit it out?" she encouraged Jenny.

Jenny rose up, nervously plucking at the fringe of her silver-gray promenade gown.

"I—you have been so kind, and I just realized—my coming here today was a—a piece of the greatest impertinence. I had no right—being sick in your parlor and getting ready to insult you. P-pray excuse me—"

The door burst open and Lizzie sailed in with an elaborate silver tea tray, which she placed on the low table in front of the sofa.

"Anything else, Madam?" she asked in a high cockney whine.

"I'll call you if I need you."

"Deafen me is more like," muttered the maid, sliding out the door.

Mrs. Maxwell laughed good-naturedly and said to Jenny as she poured, "Would you like milk and sugar, my lady, or perhaps a slice of lemon?"

"A slice of lemon?"

"I lived with a Russian dancer once," said Mrs. Maxwell. "He taught me to drink my tea that way. In a glass instead of a cup and with a slice of lemon. What a man!" she reminisced dreamily. "Real enjoyable it was."

Jenny had no idea whether she meant the man or the tea.

"Of course, it was soon after that I met Davey's father," she continued hastily, "and then I gave it up. Fenton said tea in a glass was a foreign abomination. But I always had the notion," she laughed contentedly, "that he was just jealous of poor Ivan Ivanovich."

Jenny, her head reeling, grasped at the one fragment of this amazing speech that had meaning for her. "Davey's father," she repeated. "You knew Davey's father?"

Mrs. Maxwell opened her mouth wide, displaying suspiciously white and perfect teeth. "You might put it that way, dearie. I knew him, as the saying goes, in the biblical sense."

"You mean, you were—Davey—Lord David's father was your—you were—"

"Lord bless us, you *are* new to the game, aren't you, dearie? There's no secret about it. I lived under Colby Fenton's protection for six—no, come to think of it, it was closer to seven years."

"Then you and Davey—you and David—"

"Davey was a fine, understanding boy and never looked down on me at all. A midshipman he was when our affair began, and his mother was two years dead. Colby was a good man but just a little on the weak side. Between you and me, dearie, he not only needed a woman in his bed, but he was the kind who needed one to tell him when it was time to change his nightshirt or come in out of the rain. I think Davey understood that, and he was grateful to me, not just for taking care of his pa when he was away so much but because I wasn't one of those harpies trying to suck the life's blood out of a man."

She heaved a huge sigh of satisfaction.

"Davey was never one to forget his friends.

Even after his pa died, he never visited London but he came to see me, always bringing a fine gift from them foreign parts." She nodded briskly. "I lent him a bit of what I had laid by in my stocking when he started his shipping company, and he paid me back handsomely. Then, when the company got into trouble, I helped him out again, and he insisted I take more stock. It will all go back to him one day, of course—who else do I have to leave it to—but, in the meantime, here I am living like a queen, and Lord David Fenton visits me like I was one of his fine friends whenever he's in London town, so why should I be surprised if he sends a ladyship to visit me, too?"

She bent over, looking up into Jenny's face.

"Am I right, Lady Melville? Were you wanting advice about a protector?"

"Yes," said Jenny and burst into tears.

"Don't take on like that, dearie. It's true I'm a bit out of touch these days, but that doesn't mean I can't help you out. In the meantime, if it's a roof over your head you need till you can get yourself settled, Lord bless me, there's a dozen empty rooms upstairs and me rattling about in this house with just a cook and a couple of maids. Anyone Lord David sends to me is more than welcome, and the truth is, dearie, I would enjoy having you here for myself. That is," she paused delicately, "if a ladyship like you would be willing?"

Seeing Jenny's vigorous nod, she perked up amazingly.

"And if you'll forgive the presumption, my lady—"

"Call me Jenny," interrupted her ladyship.

"Well, then, Jenny, I'm here to tell you, there's no one better able to advise you how to get on—in this business."

"That's not—exactly what I w-want," gulped Jenny, not quite able to look Mrs. Maxwell in the eye.

"But you said—"

Jenny cleared her throat loudly, but the three words still came out more like a squeak. "I want Davey."

"If you know him—if he sent you to me—?"

"I know him, but," Jenny squirmed around on the brocade seat and decided to be as honest as the situation permitted, "but *he* didn't really send me to you. You see, I had heard of you, and I thought, well, it's this way," she continued doggedly, "Lord David knew my husband and respected him a great deal, and he knows my family, too, which is very—very—Our kind of people are expected to *marry*," she explained apologetically, "not —not—"

"No need to draw any pictures, dearie,"

Mrs. Maxwell told her cheerfully. "I understand."

"He's just never thought of me that way."

"So our job is to change his way of thinking about you. Jenny, my dearie, stop your fretting. It should be as easy as stealing pennies from a blind man."

Chapter Twenty-two

MRS. THURSTON, THE HOUSEKEEPER AT MEL-
ville House, was usually the most placid of
souls, but after ten minutes of inquisitorial
questioning by the Earl of Denby, even her
usual dignified calm was considerably ruffled.

"I assure you, my lord," she told him somewhat sharply, "I have answered all your
questions truthfully, as Mr. Wickersham directed."

Lord David restrained his impatience and
tried belatedly for tact. "I don't doubt that for
a moment, Mrs. Thurston," he told her soothingly. "I just thought there was something you
might have forgotten. It seems so odd for
Je—Lady Melville to have gone away just now
when—when I was expected," he added with
sudden inspiration.

Mrs. Thurston unbent slightly. "I am sure
Lady Melville will send you a message as soon
as possible," she offered placatingly.

"She tends to be a little forgetful," Lord David murmured and gave the housekeeper a smile of great charm. "If you could just tell me once more—"

The housekeeper rolled her eyes heavenward as though imploring celestial protection against the vagaries of the nobility. Then she recited with weary patience, "Three days ago on Friday, Lady Melville went to pay a call on a friend. She did not mention her friend's name, and the brougham and coachman were hired since her own carriage is in Brighton."

"You don't happen to know where the coach was hired?"

"No, my lord, I do not. Nor even if she used the same one on her return early in the afternoon. By the time she sent for me, the footman had already carried out the one small trunk that Peggy packed for her. She then merely informed me that her friend was having family difficulties and she was going to stay with her for a few days or, at the most, a week. She did not take her maid with her."

"There was no message left for any callers?"

"Only that she was not at home, my lord, and business matters, as usual, could be referred to Mr. Wickersham."

"My dear Lord David," said Mr. Wickersham in great distress three-quarters of an

hour later. "I promise you that I am not prevaricating. If Lady Melville had informed me
of her whereabouts but requested concealment, I would undoubtedly respect her wishes. This is not the case. Although she almost
always informs me where she may be
reached, this time she did not."

An explosion of temper seemed imminent,
and recalling certain incidents in Liverpool as
well as noticing the strain His Lordship was
under, Mr. Wickersham's sympathies reached
out to him.

"It is unusual, I admit, but Her Ladyship
has not been the same since she saw you," the
lawyer added quietly.

Lord David, who had already moved toward
the door, made a sharp turn back.

"I beg your pardon."

"Evidently, you bring out certain strong
emotions in Lady Melville."

"I do?" said Lord David somewhat doubtfully. Then a broad smile broke through the
gritted teeth and the taut lips. "Do I, indeed?"

"Almost certainly, my lord, which is not a
thing I have ever observed before, and I have
seen my lady through a great deal."

They stared across at each other for a moment, the lawyer's expression grave and kindly, the Earl of Denby serious again and
breathing rather rapidly.

Then Lord David fumbled in his card case and put a card on the desk. "If you hear of anything that would help—"

The lawyer bowed slightly. "I shall inform you at once, my lord."

"I am obliged to you."

With an abrupt nod, he was out of the office and down the steep flight of stairs, waving an umbrella to summon a hackney.

"Bow Street," he told the coachman, sitting upright to avoid the stained cushions.

Why, after so many years, a few days seemed of such importance, he could not say, but so it was. Jenny might return to Melville House by tomorrow or Mr. Wickersham could come up with information this afternoon. In the meantime, it could do no harm, and perhaps himself a great deal of good—if he was to keep from going out of his mind—to have a few discreet inquiries made.

While all this anxious speculation was under way, an impenitent Jenny had been enjoying herself hugely as Mrs. Maxwell's guest and pupil.

If nothing else, she told herself, making ready for bed at the end of the first day, I should have material for a new chapter in my book.

She mentioned as much to Mrs. Maxwell over a hearty breakfast the next morning. "I ought to write a tract," she said, spreading marmalade on a piece of toast. "'The Do's and Don't's of Becoming a Courtesan.' I had no idea it was such a complicated business."

"Business is the key word," said Mrs. Maxwell sagely, "and just like in any other business, Jenny dearie, there's a buyer and a seller. First you have to sell the merchandise, but that's only the beginning. After that you've got to keep the buyer satisfied so he keeps coming back for more."

Jenny laughed so hard at this ingenuous explanation that her toast went down the wrong way. She gasped and choked, tears spurting from her eyes, while a glass of water was held to her lips and Mrs. Maxwell thumped her back.

Still coughing slightly, Jenny accompanied her hostess through the garden and back to the gazebo, where, said Mrs. Maxwell practically, there would be no danger of their being overheard.

"Lizzie does like to keep her ear to the keyhole," she mentioned tolerantly, "which mostly doesn't bother me, but *you'll* want your affairs private."

"Make that singular," murmured Jenny.

"I beg your pardon, dearie."

"I am thinking in terms of just one affair."

Mrs. Maxwell laughed delightedly. "You are one for joking," she declared. "I never thought a lady could be so—so—"

"Human?" Jenny suggested.

Mrs. Maxwell pondered the word seriously, then shook her head. "No, natural," she said as they stepped into the gazebo. "So ladylike and so natural, both together, besides which, you are beautiful. Lord David is bound to find you irresistible."

Jenny's brows climbed her forehead skeptically as she sat down on a bench and gazed in thoughtful silence at her clasped hands.

"You're forgetting what I said, Jenny, about it being a business like any other," Mrs. Maxwell reminded her, thinking she needed encouragement. "Just think about a diamond displayed in a store window so it stands out from all the other jewels, fairly begging some buyer to crave it desperately."

"I'm to be the diamond David craves?"

"Oh, you're a diamond all right, dearie; the problem to work out is how do we give you a proper setting? The time and the situation are important." She waved both plump hands. "It would be easy enough to dress you up like Princess Alice and use some excuse to bring Davey here, seeing as how he knows you so well, but it would lack excitement. We've got to shake him up a bit, make him see you in a different light from what he ever has before. It's a pity," she said regretfully, "that you can't ride well. If he could come upon you suddenly at the Achilles statue—now, that's the effect I'm looking for."

"Why would it shake him up to see me at the Achilles statue?" asked Jenny, puzzled. "And if it's horses you mean, I've been riding since I was six years old."

"Glory!" said Mrs. Maxwell, her palms smacking together. "Do you ride really well? Do you look handsome on a horse?"

"I'm considered to have light hands and a good seat," Jenny admitted, "but—"

"Then that's the way we go," exulted Mrs. Maxwell. "And if *you* can't give every pretty horse breaker in the group a run for her money, Molly Maxwell's not my name and Victoria's not the Queen of England. But there now," she said, looking at Jenny's bewildered face, "you really don't know what I'm talking about, do you?"

"I'm afraid not."

"Women riders—professionals—get paid by the West End livery stables to break horses to the side-saddle. Many of these professional riders have such appeal that for quite a few years now the men of the gentry—and the aristocracy, too—have been choosing their mistresses from among them. I think it was the newspapers that started the custom of calling them the pretty horse breakers. It's caused some of them to do quite well—why,

Hartington gave Skittles—she's the best of the
lot—two thousand pounds a year—and now
those same papers complain that the horse
breakers have pushed their way into society.
They have, too!" she added, not without pride.
"They wear real flashy outfits and ride real
fine horse flesh, and there's not one of them
with any pretense to looks who, when she
shows herself at the statue, doesn't manage
sooner or later to get herself a good offer."

"That's the Achilles statue you mentioned?" Jenny asked, her mind turning over
the possibilities.

"Yes, in Hyde Park. It's the gathering spot
for them all, and I know for a fact it's where
Lord David met Naomi two years ago."

"Naomi?"

Mrs. Maxwell watched Jenny's smiling blue
eyes turn cool and green. She felt unaccounta-
bly embarrassed.

"It didn't last long, d-dearie," she stuttered.
"It never does. She's a greedy, grasping sort of
girl. Davey is generous, but he's not a fool."

She gathered by Jenny's expression that she
had not improved the situation and wisely
stopped trying. "Lord David rides in the park
every day, weather permitting, when he's in
London," she stated calmly. "If you are sure
you want to attract him, I don't think you
could do better than to arrange a meeting in
the park."

"Oh, I most definitely want to attract him," muttered Jenny with a look in her eye that boded Lord David no good.

Mrs. Maxwell chose to ignore the look. She was staring at Jenny and suddenly jumped up to take the combs and pins out of her hair, tumbling it all down around her face and over her shoulders.

"Green!" she exclaimed. "An emerald green riding habit. I saw just what I have in mind at my dressmaker's only last week. I'll send her a note as soon as we get back to the house. With your coloring and eyes it would be perfect. No hat—that's an important touch because they all wear fancy hats. Instead, you'll have your hair all carefully curled and disordered the way it is right now. I suppose you know, dearie, you've got hair that could fairly make a man wild to see it all laid out on a pillow?"

"N-no," said Jenny, swallowing. "I didn't know."

"Lord, dearie, your husband must have been a—"

Just in time she bit back the rather salty comment on her lips and substituted, "Don't think Davey won't notice. He will right off. Take it from me, there's not much about women that one doesn't notice," she advised with relish. "Well, will you do it, Jenny, my dearie, or have you had second thoughts?"

"An emerald-green riding habit and my hair all down," mused Jenny. "What about the horse?"

"One of them red-brown creatures to go with your hair," said Mrs. Maxwell promptly.

"Chestnut."

"That's it, chestnut. I'll send word to a livery stable owner in the West End. Fenton used to stable with him. If he doesn't have what we want, he'll know where to get it. A week's rental, say?"

"If you think one week would be enough."

Mrs. Maxwell's eyes twinkled roguishly. "We'll plan on a week, but Jenny, dearie, once he catches sight of you tricked out the way I plan, and knows that you're available, unless I'm not the judge I used to be, one minute should be enough!"

Chapter Twenty-three

ALTERATIONS TO THE EMERALD-GREEN RIDING dress took longer than expected, so another three days were to pass before Jenny made her sensational debut at the Achilles statue in Hyde Park.

The jacket of her habit had a high, Hussar-style còllar with two rows of small military buttons down the front, exaggerated shoulders, but such a tight fit over the bust and at the waist that it was like being sewn into a second skin, Jenny complained breathlessly.

"You can't expect to set a fashion and be comfortable, too, dearie," Mrs. Maxwell told her philosophically. And when Jenny looked into the dressmaker's mirror at her final fitting, she was forced to agree.

The emerald riding habit turned her eyes to a brilliant, sparkling green; it gave her a figure that David—most men, she amended to herself, wetting her suddenly dry lips with the tip of her tongue—would go wild to see in the flesh.

When the chestnut mare chosen by Mr. Chadderton was trotted out for her inspection at his West End livery stable the afternoon before her launching as a pretty horse breaker, Jenny was equally satisfied with the horse.

"Oh, what a beauty!" she cried.

"Beauty's her name, my lady, and beauty's her nature. A fine, mettlesome creature, too."

His eyes swiveled between the red-brown mare and the lady with the fox-red hair.

Two of a kind, his looks told Jenny as plainly as though he had said the words aloud, and she smiled to herself, hoping her reception at the statue would be equally complimentary.

She was less pleased the next day with Ferguson, the groom assigned to her at her request. He seemed to be the very stereotype of the dour Scotsman, ruggedly good-looking despite the perpetual scowl on his face, fiery-haired, and bad-tempered.

"You do know what you're supposed to do, Ferguson?" she asked him nervously, settling her full skirts gracefully about Beauty after he had helped her to mount.

"Aye." He swung up into the saddle of his own black stallion. "Trail alongside you like a tame lackey," he told her sourly, "and see you no' get into trouble."

Jenny stared at him in haughty displeasure.

"If you find the prospect too onerous," she said, "I can ask Mr. Chadderton to give me another groom."

"That you will not," said Ferguson. "I trained Beauty, and I stay with her. Let's be going then."

"You trained Beauty to the side-saddle?" said Jenny sweetly to his rigid back, a pleasantry he did not deign to answer.

"Well, you can ride, I'll say that for you," he told her grudgingly as they passed through Stanhope Gate, "and you're no' overfond of the spur and the whip like some of the fine ladies and gentlemen who flatter themselves overmuch they know how to control a beast."

"I take it," said Jenny, lips twitching, "I have just received high praise?"

"Aye," he said, "on your *horsemanship*." The emphasis was very obvious.

"Do you disapprove of me, Ferguson?" she asked him with unconcealed amusement.

"It's not my place to disapprove, my lady," he said austerely, then seemed unable to resist adding, "but if you were my sister, you'd not be able to sit yon horse or any other, your backside would be too sore."

"Ferguson, how dare you!"

"If you're no wanting proper answers, then do not be asking the questions." He pointed with his crop. "Just ahead at the gathering of the crowd is where you're wanting to go."

"The Achilles statue?"

He scowled fiercely. "The same."

Jenny straightened in the saddle, set Beauty at a canter, and rode toward the crowd, Ferguson just behind her. When she arrived near the statue, she slowed again to a walk and imperiously beckoned Ferguson to ride beside her.

Although pretending not to be, she was completely conscious of the wide-eyed stares, the whispers, the gaping mouths, the admiring spectators, the jealous looks of women who might be competitors, and the avid, interested looks of the mounted men in their top hats who might be prospective protectors.

Giving them all a good chance to view her—enviously or covetously, as the case might be—she then proceeded, with Ferguson trailing behind her, along Rotten Row, where more than one man mishandled his team at the sudden sight of her.

Public reaction was all that Jenny could have desired, except for one thing. The diamond had been polished to perfection and placed strategically in a shop window, but Lord David was not among the shoppers. After an hour she returned to the stable and, from there, for the first time, went home to Melville House.

Mrs. Thurston greeted her with glad cries of

surprise and a slightly exaggerated report of Lord David's displeasure at her continued stay away from home and the importunity of his visits.

"Will you be at home to him now, my lady?"

"No," said Jenny, trying to sound casual. "Tell him, if you please, that I am much occupied but can be found every morning between ten and eleven riding in Hyde Park."

"Hyde Park, my lady, is a fair-sized place."

Her lady debated whether she should mention the statue and decided on a compromise. "Along Rotten Row," she specified and went upstairs to pen a note to Mrs. Maxwell.

Late in the afternoon and all during the evening it rained hard, and Jenny uttered more than one prayer for the weather to improve by the next day.

Heaven favored her with a crisply cool but sunny morning, and she was just coming downstairs with the skirt of her emerald-green habit slung over her arm when the door knocker sounded.

She heard footsteps along the marbled hallway and hung back out of sight. Sure enough, her premonition was correct. That clear, incisive voice could belong to no one else. There was a short, sharp exchange of words, a pause, another exchange, and then the closing of the door.

To be safe, Jenny stayed upstairs waiting. Mrs. Thurston, puffing up the stairs, found her mistress sitting quietly on the top step.

"Lord David has been and gone, m'lady," she panted. "Collins told him you had returned from your visit but were not at home, so he demanded to see me. I told him you had left the house a quarter of an hour ago to go riding in the park."

"Marvelous," said Jenny, jumping up and almost tumbling down the stairs in her eagerness. "Now I had better make it true," she flung over her shoulder as Mrs. Thurston came hurrying after her.

Forty minutes later, Ferguson, even more dour than the day before, was helping her onto Beauty. In scowling silence, he mounted his black stallion and followed Jenny out of the stable.

Jenny's heart beat fast in mingled hope and dread as once more they approached the Achilles statue.

Some of the spectators from the day before shouted out their recognition along with good-natured compliments. Jenny smiled and tossed her hair back, deliberately allowing part of the swirling red mass to settle onto her shoulders.

"And what's your name, love?" shouted a woman in the crowd.

"Aye, love, tell us your name!" echoed a man.

Jenny leaned forward to pat Beauty's mane. When she straightened up again, offering an obvious display of her figure in the skin-tight emerald green, there was a concerted sigh, then a smattering of cheers.

Lord David Fenton, just passing by the statue after two trips up and down the Row in search of the elusive Lady Melville, wheeled his bay about, paused to greet a friend, and almost dropped his reins.

Jenny!

He did not know later whether he had whispered her name or shouted it or only echoed it in his own mind.

Jenny it was, hanging out at the Achilles statue, dressed no differently from one of the pretty horse breakers in a flashy emerald green and not so much as a scarf, let alone a hat on her head.

How dare she wear her hair in that boudoir style for all the world to see? How dare she smile at the eager crowd and the bold-eyed men, as though—by God, didn't she know what they would think? But, of course, she knew. Jenny always knew what she was doing. His hands tightened on the reins of his horse, which moved forward uneasily.

Jenny had spotted Lord David among the

riders at the exact moment he first saw her. She had not lost sight of him after that, not for a second. Now, as the woman in the crowd shrilled once again, "Come on, love, tell us your name," she pretended to ignore the man circling the crowd on his big bay in order to reach her.

"Sure and I'm a green rose from Ireland," she called out to the crowd in a rich, thick brogue.

Lord David heard and, when his first rage passed, "I'll throttle her!" he told himself dispassionately.

Ferguson heard and wheeled his horse about to come alongside her. "Woman!" he told her. "You're making a spectacle of yourself. Come away with you."

Lord David was almost upon them; it was the moment she had been longing for, waiting for, and working to achieve. Her heart should have soared up in triumph; instead it seemed lodged in her breast, cutting off her breath.

The closer he got, the more clearly she could see him. His face was pale with anger, and cold fury threatened her from his black eyes. His brows, drawn together in as ferocious a scowl as Ferguson's, set her shuddering.

Not in obedience but in sudden panic, she responded to the touch of the Scots groom's hand on her reins. Together their horses gathered speed. Neck by neck, they fled along

Rotten Row, and after them came the Earl of Denby, a grim-faced, avenging Pegasus.

The thundering hooves of his bay flashed past them, churning up dust and mud. A safe distance ahead, he wheeled his bay across their path, so they had no choice but to pull their own horses short before they reached him.

"Can you hold our horses?" Lord David demanded of Ferguson.

The Scotsman looked him over, looked at Jenny—quite pale with fright—turned once more to Lord David, and surprisingly gave him a curt nod. "Aye," he said, "I can."

Lord David leaped down from his horse, thrusting the reins at Ferguson. He came over to Jenny. "Get down," he ordered her, and she slid into his waiting arms.

He let go of her immediately to grasp her elbow and pull her off the path and against the trunk of a huge oak. "Now," said Lord David between his teeth, making no attempt to lower his voice. "Now tell me what the hell are you up to, Jenny?"

"Up to?" Jenny hedged, and was promptly seized hold of and shaken furiously while Ferguson, three feet away, nodded approval.

"Answer me, damn you! Mingling with the horse breakers, dressed and acting like a woman of the demi-monde. Do you want all of London to mistake you for a courtesan?"

"I don't mind," smiled Jenny, no longer frightened or panicky.

"Wh-what!" He was so startled that he let go of her.

"I stopped caring what people think of me a long time ago, except for the few, the very few I respect. Sir Charles taught me independence and gave me the means to maintain it. My mother taught me it is better to live in happiness as a mistress than in misery as a wife."

"Is that why you refused me—because of your mother?"

"I refused you because of *me*, David. Myself alone. What have I to gain by marrying you? A title. I'm already 'my lady.' Money? I have as much, far more than I will ever need. Protection? The men in my life—except Sir Charles —have not been notable for taking care of me. I can do better for myself. Lovemaking? It doesn't require a wedding ring and a license to have that."

She clasped both hands at the back of her neck, spilling her hair back over her shoulders, the silky mass of hair Mrs. Maxwell had said most men would love to see laid out on a pillow.

Watching David's distracted reaction to her gesture, even in the midst of his anger, she suspected that Mrs. Maxwell might be right.

"I don't think I would mind being considered of the demi-monde, David," she repeated softly. "If I become a man's wife, it's a lifetime sentence; as his mistress, I am utterly free."

"I never heard such rubbish in my life!" roared David.

Ferguson, still holding the horses, nodded violent agreement.

"Oh, dear!" said Jenny. "And here I was considering you for my list."

"What list?" shouted David and Ferguson together.

"The list of men whose mistress I might be," answered Jenny artlessly. "Oh, dear!" she said again. "And I quite thought, Lord David, that I would like you for my lover."

Chapter Twenty-four

THEY RODE SEDATELY THROUGH THE PARK, three abreast, exiting by way of Marble Arch so as to avoid returning past the Achilles statue. Jenny rode, not by her choice, in the middle, with Lord David's bay and Ferguson's stallion nudging Beauty far too closely on either side for her rider to even contemplate escaping her two guards.

It was a notion Jenny had not considered for a moment, her first flurry of panic having completely evaporated. She felt the advantage had returned to her and was enjoying herself hugely, amused at rather than apprehensive of the current of disapproval crackling between her and the groom in about the same proportion as the anger and exasperation emanating from Lord David.

When they arrived at Chadderton's livery stable, Lord David said to Ferguson, ignoring

Jenny, "I am taking Lady Melville home. Can you stable my horse for a few hours? I'll send a groom for him later."

"I can take myself home," Jenny announced.

The Scotsman ignored her, too.

"Aye," he said to the earl and added with a certain grudging respect, "I'll see to him myself, me lord."

"Get down," Lord David told Jenny just as he had in the park.

She frowned a little at his imperious tone but once again slid down into his outstretched arms.

In the hired carriage on their way to Melville House, he sat in the farthest corner away from her, his arms crossed over his chest.

"So you prefer to be my mistress rather than my wife, Jenny?" he asked agreeably.

Jenny mistrusted that pleasant manner.

"It's not personal," she answered carefully. "At this point in my life, I expect—it just seems better for me to be any man's mistress rather than his wife. I have so much more to gain by remaining unwed."

"For instance?" he queried softly.

Jenny took several deep, forced breaths. "Well, David, let us say I chose to marry you. At our wedding, along with pledging me your eternal love and devotion, you would promise to endow me with all your worldly goods. The reality of marriage is quite contrary to the supposedly sacred vows that are made."

She paused, and Lord David said ironically, "I have yielded you the floor."

"We both know how long promises of love and devotion last; we pledged them once, remember?"

Seeing his face pale, she bit her lip and hurried on. "My real concern, however, is with more practical matters. Today I am the second largest shareholder in Irish Rose. The day I wed you, my shares would belong to you. So would every other share and investment I possess and all my monies. I would be in the position of having to ask you to give me what is my own. You could sell Melville House from under me if you chose; you could close down my convalescing home in Brighton. You could take the monies I earn by Sir Charles's books and my own, or even, if you so desired, refuse to allow their publication."

"You assume," he asked with awful irony, "knowing my dissolute, profligate nature, that I would do all those things?"

"No," said Jenny, more honest than she had been with him in years, "I assume you would deal with me like the decent, honorable gentleman you are."

"Then what the hell is all the fuss about?"

"The fuss is about your legal right to act

other than honorably, if you so desire. Why," she demanded excitedly, "should I or any woman be at the mercy of a husband's willingness to do what is right or wrong? Why should the marriage ceremony turn wives into legal infants?"

"You were willing to marry me five years ago."

"Seven years ago, if you must know." She gave a bitter little laugh. "From the first night we met—I was not yet sixteen, remember?—I would have crawled from Somerset to the dock at Portsmouth on my hands and knees for the chance to wed you. You, David, Lieutenant. Fenton, not even a captain yet, certainly not the Earl of Derby. I loved you so much—so much—then."

Remembered bitterness of his own came pouring out of him. "Yet two years later when I asked you to come away with me—"

"I had promised my mother. I really believed I was acting in your best interests."

"The promise was easily made," he sneered, "perhaps as easily as you gulled yourself into believing what you wanted to believe."

Unexpected tears stung her eyes. She blinked them back, willing her voice steady. "I'll tell you a little secret, David. It shows you what a fool I was, but after this long time it hardly matters. The day after we quarreled and parted, I went down to the stables early in the morning, having hardly slept all night. Our groom, Jim, saddled my horse and promised to keep it secret that I had ridden over to the Carrolls. I planned to throw pebbles at your window to awaken you and bring you down to me. I wanted to tell you that no one mattered but you, nothing but us. I would break my promise to Mama, I would let Sir Lewis disown me, I would allow you to take on the burden of providing for a penniless wife. I would have gone with you that moment, if you would have had me, in nothing but my riding habit and boots."

She shrugged. "Of course, you weren't there to have me, David. You had taken yourself off with your pride and resentment for company. As you yourself once admitted, you left me when I needed you without a backward look."

Lord David's arms were no longer crossed; his fists were clenched against his knees.

"It's rather inadequate," he muttered after a while, "to say that I'm sorry, Jenny—that I've been sorry for all these long years."

"Oh, never fear," she mocked herself as well as him, "my heart didn't break. I discovered that, contrary to novels, hearts do not. They get a bit sore and bruised, perhaps, but one survives. Sometimes," she laughed, almost happily this time, "one survives very well. I did.

"Still, one can't go back, David. Surely you can see that? I'm not little infatuated Jenny Rosellen any more. I'm Janet Melville, Sir Charles's widow, a woman of wealth and independence. I can make my own rules. I can lead my own life."

"No one is ever completely free to do that, Jenny," he told her quietly. "Not even an earl. We all have our obligations. Society has its rules."

"Society may cast me out with my good will," Jenny told him cheerfully. "It won't throw *you* out, David. If a gentleman takes a mistress, he is considered a fine, dashing fellow, doing what gentlemen do naturally. It's only the lady taking a lover who is condemned and shunned. Such hypocrites we Victorians are!"

"The queen enjoyed such marital happiness before Prince Albert's death that—"

"Oh, stuff! The queen may have adored Albert, though I sometimes wonder—I find her excessive mourning suspicious—but I can tell you, as a woman, she did not enjoy bearing him nine children in seventeen years. I have been several times in company with one of her former ladies of the bedchamber, and even while Her Majesty was railing aloud against women's rights, she was admitting privately that men are very selfish beings and the submission demanded of the female makes our sex unenviable. Are you laughing at me?"

"If I don't laugh, Jenny, I will cry." He then proceeded to do both, laughing so hard that tears spurted out of his eyes. "From a proposal of marriage in a Somerset cemetery, which you spurned indignantly—and, yes, thank you, I am recovered from the twisted knee I received when you shoved me down on a tombstone—we wound up in a dirty office overlooking the Mersey River making love on a desk."

"*Almost* making love," Jenny reminded him rather tartly.

"No, Jenny," he corrected her. "We were definitely making love. The hors d'oeuvres and removes and flans may not be considered the main course, but they are definitely part of the meal. Unfortunately, as it now turns out," he told her pleasantly, "we did not quite finish our meal."

Jenny, to her chagrin, blushed a bright hot crimson, and the earl continued affably, "I tried to find an opportunity in both Liverpool and London to renew my proposals. When I finally did locate you in Hyde Park, you were there aping a would-be society courtesan. We commence from your offer to become my mistress and wind up discussing women's rights and the queen's sexual attitudes. I don't know whether I am laughing at you or at myself or perhaps at both of us, but under the circumstances I have no choice, I suppose, but to consider your inviting offer."

"How noble of you!"

"Well, Lady Melville, it is rather, don't you know, considering that I have had all the mistresses I want? Indeed, I would like to dispose permanently of the lot of them in favor of a wife and—forgive me if this offends you—children."

"To be sure. Lots of little lords for the earldom."

"Just one or two would have satisfied me," he stated calmly, "and, of course, at least one little girl with foxfire curls."

Jenny's hand went instinctively to the tumbled mass of her hair. Her lips quivered.

Lord David continued in the same tranquil way, "I have a dinner engagement tonight and some business affairs in the morning. Will you dine with me tomorrow night, Jenny, at the Blue Post in Cork Street? The food is more than adequate, and I can secure a snug private parlor on the ground floor."

Seeing her momentary hesitation, he continued smoothly, "If we come to an agreement, in future you may be able to dine at my house. I have a French chef who is little short of a genius and should delight you if you have as healthy an appetite as formerly. Do you?"

"There is still nothing I enjoy more than a good meal," Jenny said hurriedly, then blushed again with mortification when he chuckled.

"Your poor husband," he told her with kindly mockery. "I hope soon to have you amend that declaration."

"Shall I meet you at the restaurant?" Jenny asked quickly for something, anything, to say.

"I will send my carriage for you at half past seven."

"Thank you," said Jenny.

"You are welcome. And Jenny?"

"My lord?"

"You will not go to the Achilles statue tomorrow."

"Is that a command?"

"No, my dear. I hope I know better than to command you. It is more—shall we say—an entreaty. I do not wish you to receive any other offers until you have dealt with mine in form."

"Very well."

"Good." The earl crossed his arms again, tipped his hat over his face, and leaned back, eyes closed.

"No, Jenny," he said after a minute, not troubling to open his eyes. "I am not asleep, merely resting. Chasing after you has proved a tiring, not to say tiresome business. Perhaps," he added musingly, "if we become lovers, I may get more rest. Now there's an attractive thought."

"Go to the devil!" snapped Jenny as the carriage stopped before Melville House.

Chapter Twenty-five

THE EARL, VERY CORRECTLY DRESSED IN A black cutaway and a white satin waistcoat, was waiting at the entrance of the Blue Post when Jenny arrived in his carriage.

He helped her out and escorted her inside to their private parlor, waved away the assistance of the maitre d', and himself removed her satin damask cloak.

For a moment he looked her over, silently admiring. Her gown of amber silk billowed out over extra-wide hoops to emphasize the slenderness of her waist. A single row of small bows decorated the bodice; the neckline was trimmed with pleated tulle. An amber necklace hung about her white throat, its gold pendant dangling just above the swell of her breasts.

"You are beautiful, Jenny," murmured the earl when the maitre d' had departed to fetch some sherry.

"You mean my gown, I collect?"

"I mean *you*," said the earl, coming up behind her to catch hold of her bare shoulders and turn her about, his eyes boldly raking her from waist to throat.

A waiter entered with their wine, and while they sipped it Jenny asked him baldly, "Shall we have our discussion now?"

"Presently," said Lord David easily. "After we eat. There is plenty of time, and we can be more private then."

With two waiters serving them, for the next hour there was no privacy at all as course succeeded course, first turtle soup followed by oyster and lobster patties, then a roast, next stuffed pheasant with vegetables, sauces and sweets, and a variety of fine wines for every dish.

Their conversation was desultory and impersonal while they ate, the earl contributing anecdotes on his experiences in the House of Lords, Jenny telling him her plans for the convalescing home, and, as she emptied glass after glass he signaled the waiter to pour for her, speaking more frankly of her book on women, wives, and whores.

"Oh, my, I'm so stuffed!" she said, dabbling her fingers in the bowl of scented water proffered by one waiter while the other cleared away the remains on the table.

"Surely," Lord David smiled across from

her, "you are not going to forego dessert. The tarts are delicious here, I understand, and the cakes—"

"Well," said Jenny weakly, and with the maitre d' adding his persuasion to Lord David's, she succumbed to cherries flambèe.

Lord David then dismissed the waiters and himself poured their apricot liqueur.

"To us, Jenny," he toasted her.

"To us," Jenny agreed and smiled at him fuzzily.

"Drink your liqueur, Jenny."

"I think I'm tipsy enough already."

"It's not a toast unless you drink."

"All right," said Jenny, and she gulped the liqueur down in one long swallow. She smiled happily across at him, setting the empty glass on the rocking table. "Do we talk now or go to bed?"

"*You* go to bed, Jenny. Alone."

"Without you?"

"Without me."

"That doesn't sound like much fun," Jenny sulked.

"No, it doesn't," sighed Lord David, "but, you see, Jenny, I've grown into a conservative —you'd probably call it stuffy—kind of fellow. Maybe it's this damn earldom. Whatever—I can't see my way clear to taking you for my mistress. If you want to share my bed, my dear, you are going to have to do it with a ring around your finger."

Jenny reached out and clutched with both hands at the table, which now seemed to be sashaying up and down. So was her chair.

"Then—then—I'll have to—just have to bed —with someone—'nother man," she enunciated with some difficulty.

"Not bloody likely," the Earl of Denby pronounced grimly and caught her neatly in his arms as her head fell forward and she slid sideways off her chair.

Jenny tried to open her eyes and found it a task beyond her strength. She lay quite still for some time, indignantly aware that someone was tapping on her forehead with the blunt end of a hammer. However delicate the strokes, they nevertheless sent waves of agony along the back of her head and down her neck.

Making a supreme effort, she opened her eyes to bid her torturer to desist and found that she was alone. Bright sunlight pouring through one tiny window in an otherwise gloomy little room sent further twinges of pain rippling through her eyeballs. The hammering appeared to be internal.

She lay quite still, trying to bring her mind and memory into focus.

It all came back to her at last. Dinner with

Lord David in a private parlor at the Blue Post. Stuffing herself. All those glasses of wine—she shuddered in remembrance. Cherries flambèe—she hadn't finished them—and the toast with apricot liqueur. Lord David refusing to have her for his mistress, saying she had to go to bed alone.

With a little moan of anguish, Jenny sat upright, her hands on either side of her face to hold her head in place.

She was in bed alone and very chastely garbed in a high-necked nightdress of pale pink muslin buttoned with tiny cloth buttons. Jenny squinted at the bell sleeves with their fine fall of lace over her wrists.

Be damned if it wasn't her own nightgown; she had chosen that lace herself. But this was not her own bed, certainly not her own room or her house.

By degrees she moved her seemingly paralyzed legs around till they were capable of bending, with her feet flat on the bare wood floor. Then she staggered erect, padded over to the door, and gave it a vigorous tug. Then another one.

Locked! She was locked in!

"Hey!" she shouted. "Open up and let me out of here!"

She went reeling back at the shock of hearing her voice. It was like being imprisoned in a carillon tower while the bells pealed about her.

Supporting her head again so it would not unhinge from her body, she took the perilous six-foot journey back to the bed.

She must have dozed for a few minutes because she heard neither the door open or close nor footsteps approaching on the uncarpeted floor.

"Good morning," said Lord David cheerily. "Did you call?"

She opened one baleful eye, then the other, and gave him a look that might have terrified a less resolute man than the Earl of Denby.

"Where am I?" she demanded, pulling herself up and crawling down to the foot of the bed.

"In a friend's untenanted house about twenty miles from London."

"When? How? For God's sake, why?" For her own sake, she spoke her demanding words softly.

Lord David fetched the single wicker chair the room boasted and set it down next to the bed. He sat in it, very much at his ease, and casually crossed tweed-trousered legs.

"It's really very simple, Jenny," he said, smiling at her benignly. "I drugged your liqueur after supper last night to make it easier to abduct you."

"Abduct me! Why, you—you—"

"Bastard?" he suggested helpfully.

"Bloody, rotten, stinking bastard. Why?"

With each added unfavorable adjective, Lord David's grin had deepened. "Behold, not the Earl of Denby," he answered good-humoredly, "but young Lochinvar. Or should I say not-so-young Lochinvar?"

"You're mad," Jenny told him with conviction. "You're a raving bedlamite."

"No, my dear. I am merely a man determined on a course of action, which is to be no longer—and about time, too—a laggard in love. I want you for my wife." He smiled gently. "I mean to have you for my wife. There is a special license in my pocket, and a vicar lives a ten-minute carriage ride from here. The moment you agree to accept his services, Ferguson will fetch him to us to perform the marriage ceremony."

"Ferguson! You mean the groom from Chadderton's livery stable!" she cried out incredulously. "He knows about this."

"Aided and abetted," admitted Lord David, unabashed. "His Scots tenacity was very useful to me. He drove the carriage for the abduction. I sat inside holding you."

"What kind of bribe did you have to give him?" Jenny asked spitefully.

"None at all," said the earl nonchalantly.

"He's in my employ now, and he thoroughly approved of the abduction. In fact, if I had listened to him," he looked her over speculatively, and Jenny had a sudden scared wish she despised herself for to retreat back under the blankets, "I would be applying much more forcible methods to accomplish my ends. I believe he thinks that I'm a bit of an effete Englishman in my dealings with you. Still, he'll go along with any scheme that gets yon lassie—meaning you—to the kirk—that's church—to be respectably wedded."

"You can both wait until the devil marches up from hell!" Jenny told him in a flaming fury.

To which Lord David only inquired in great concern, "Are you hungry, Jenny?"

"No, you bastard, how can I be hungry? My head throbs, my eyes are sore, I'm sick at my stomach, and I—"

"Did I remember to tell you there's a chamberpot under the bed?" he interrupted solicitously.

"Oh, God, you—you devil. I hate you. I'll kill you for this, you—you—"

At a loss for words sufficiently vile to describe him, she ran out of breath, which was just as well. Before she could think of any, the earl had gone out of the room, not forgetting to lock the door behind him.

It was some hours later before he returned, as nearly as Jenny could determine in the early afternoon. He carried a small tray, which he set beside her on the bed.

"Feeling better, Jenny?" he asked her in apparent deep anxiety.

With great difficulty, she swallowed a pungent retort and meekly answered, "Yes."

She looked down at the tray, which contained a single cup of tea and one slice of lightly buttered bread.

"I'm a bit hungry, too, now," she acknowledged grudgingly. "I could do with something more substantial."

He looked down at her and answered with seeming regret, despite the suggestion of a smiling gleam in his eyes. "I'm sorry, Jenny, but tea and bread is all I can offer you."

"What's the matter?" she asked bitterly. "Did you forget to abduct a cook, too?"

"I didn't forget. I knew one would not be needed."

"You thought my stay here would be so short?"

"On the contrary, knowing your stubbornness, I feared it might be far too long, so I made arrangements for Ferguson and me to take our meals at the inn a few miles down the road. For your meals, Ferguson has offered to make the tea, while I," he announced with the air of a magician conjuring a rabbit out of a hat, "I will slice and butter the bread."

Jenny stared up at him, her eyes glazing over in horrified comprehension.

He appeared to understand what she was thinking.

"I'm afraid so," he told her sympathetically.

"You're going to starve me!"

"Not starve you, Jenny." He pretended hurt that she should so misjudge him. "Why, you could live for at least a week off that meal you had last night," he reminded her with gentle malice. "I hope you won't have to, of course. I've been told a person can exist quite a while on a diet of bread and water. It's probably true."

He watched her hands close convulsively around the handle of the tea cup.

"Jenny, I hope you're planning to drink that, not throw it," he urged. "There won't be a replacement until tea time."

Jenny looked down at the tea, then longingly up at the face into which she had planned to dash it.

"B-b-bastard," she said, biting savagely at the bread. "Son of a bitch," she threw in for good measure after drinking the tea.

He took the tray from her and tossed some papers onto her lap.

"Whatever you say, Jenny," and he left the room, laughing.

She heard the click of the lock when he got outside. The laughter was still in his voice when he raised it to shout through the door.

"Just the same, I'm the son of a bitch bastard you are going to marry!"

Chapter Twenty-six

AN HOUR LATER THE DOOR WAS UNLOCKED AND Lord David entered her tiny room so suddenly that Jenny had no time to descend from the wicker chair on which she stood, wielding an old brass candlestick in a fruitless attempt to knock away the wooden slats across the window.

Lord David half knelt and eased a small traveling trunk from his shoulder onto the floor. Then he came over to the chair.

"May I help you, Jenny?" he asked with calm courtesy, holding out his hand.

Jenny bit her lip, then cast him a glance of smoldering dislike as she accepted the hand to help her to the floor.

"I should have warned you," Lord David said politely, "that the boards were nailed across the window only yesterday. Besides being quite sturdy, they are very firmly anchored to the frame. It would take better tools, I think, and greater strength than yours to unfasten them. Especially now."

"Why especially now?"

"In view of your enterprise," he bowed as though they were chatting under the most normal of circumstances, "I shall instruct Ferguson to check the window from the outside on the hour."

He chuckled wickedly. "Were you really planning to escape in your nightdress, Lady Melville?"

"I would walk to London barefoot and naked to get out of here," Jenny panted in impotent fury and frustration.

"That won't be necessary. Should you escape, and you won't, Jenny dear," he jeered gently, "you may do so decently clad. The trunk contains your clothing. I told your maid to pack simple day wear for a two-week stay in the country, where you were providing company for a sick friend."

"You told my maid!"

"With Mrs. Thurston's permission," he hastened to assure her. "You need not worry about your staff. They all believe in the story of the sick friend. Your Peggy was a bit hurt at being left behind again, but I explained that the simple country cottage you were visiting had no accommodations for a lady's maid."

"You really planned this very thoroughly, didn't you?" Jenny asked him bitterly.

"Well, do you know, given the short amount of time I had after encountering you at the Achilles statue, I think I did," he answered with modest pride.

He looked at the bowed red head and the bare feet peeking out from under the pink muslin nightdress and had no illusions that she was defeated or even despondent. Plans for his undoing were being hatched inside the red head. The Earl of Denby knew that as surely as naval lieutenant. Fenton had known the constellations. In the meantime—"Would you like to dress, Jenny, and take a walk in the garden?" he asked her coaxingly.

Jenny lifted up her face, eyes bright with hope and interest. "I would love it," she said fervently and then sought to seem a little less eager. "This room is so stuffy, and it's so boring alone here with nothing to do," she went on in a languid society voice.

"Don't belabor it, Jenny." He grinned cheerfully. "You do understand, I hope, that you will have my humble self for companion on our walk, and we will stroll arm in arm? I have no intention of trusting you out of my sight or touch."

"I understand," Jenny said sweetly. And then, as he stood watching her, "Pray, may I have privacy to dress?" She gave him a smile brimming over with malice and mischief. "Unless you are minded to accept my offer instead of insisting that I accept yours?"

His cheeks reddened, and he resisted, not without a struggle, the ungentlemanly impulse to box both her ears.

"I shall return in fifteen minutes," said the Earl of Denby, retreating without dignity. This time *her* mocking laughter followed *him* through the door.

Jenny pawed quickly through the contents of the trunk. No useful weapons—that was too much to expect—but several serviceable dark skirts and plain blouses and her hooded navy wool cloak as well as the heavier plaid. A pair of sturdy, serviceable walking shoes as well as thinner slippers. A small cloth jewel case containing some of the lighter pieces she wore in the day—simple gold chains and bracelets and four or five brooches. Good! When she got away, she might have to put them up as surety for a coach at the inn Lord David had mentioned. Ah, her little peacock pin with the small, spreading tail of rubies, sapphires, and diamonds. Better still. Even an innkeeper should recognize its value. Her pearls. Not the valuable double rope from Sir Charles but the string of pink pearls Commander David Fenton had clasped around her neck in the Carroll rose garden.

She would never leave her precious pink pearls with any innkeeper. Even as she planned to run away from the man who had given them to her so many years before, Jenny was unaware of any inconsistency in her attitude.

It might be war of a certain kind between David and her now, each one determined to best the other, but the pearls were a symbol of the happiest six weeks of her life, six weeks when she loved him with all her heart and felt loved the same way in return.

She clasped the pearls around her neck, pulled off the muslin nightdress, slipped into a chemise and petticoats, and tugged on a pair of lisle stockings. A plain gray gown, its high neck buttoned over her pearls, and the blue cloak completed her outfit. She was ready when Lord David came for her.

"You call this a garden?" complained Jenny several minutes later as she stumbled along a narrow path overgrown with wild, unclipped hedges, clinging out of necessity to the arm thrust through hers.

Lord David bent to free her cloak from a clinging bramble.

"My friend has fallen on hard times," he said, keeping his face a careful blank. "Perhaps, with the rental money I offered him, he will be able to—er—effect some improvements."

"Improvements!" Jenny sniffed scornfully. "Not unless you paid him a king's ransom. Can't we walk along the road?" She allowed a pathetic note to creep into her voice. "This path is so hard and uneven, it hurts my feet."

"If you will promise not to speak to anyone we chance to meet."

Jenny hesitated. Then she said dulcetly, "I promise."

He eyed her carefully. "Sorry, Jenny. I don't believe you. If I know you," he added thoughtfully, "you wouldn't feel bound to keep a promise made under duress." He turned her around to face him, holding her by the waist instead of the arm. "Would you?" he demanded.

"No, damn you!" she flung at him, and his answering shout of laughter was full of pure joy.

"Oh, Jenny, you wonderful, impossible girl, I do love you," he said and pulled her into his arms and kissed her with rough exuberance. After a long while he let go of her and looked down for a moment at the still, pale face lying across his chest. Then he commenced to kiss her again.

"You would never make a living as a mistress kissing that way," he whispered in her ear after a while. "Rather I should say, *not* kissing. Even in a wife it would not be too acceptable."

Jenny's eyes opened, startling him with a look of naked, hungry passion that he had not felt on her lips.

He put her from him hurriedly, though prudently retaining a hold on her arm. This chilly garden wilderness was even less suitable for dalliance than the battered desk in the Merseyside office.

"Did you read the marriage settlement I left with you?" he asked by way of distraction, turning her back in the direction of the house.

"Is that what it was?" asked Jenny vaguely.

"I thought it was quite clear. So did Mr. Wickersham. Of course, he wants a more detailed document, but we both felt the one he drew up would serve temporarily. Didn't you understand it?"

"I suppose so."

"Damnation, Jenny, a child could have understood it. I relinquished any and all husbandly claim to anything you own—stock, property, money. I gave up all legal rights to any part of your estate whatsoever. You retain the use, management, and maintenance of your properties in any way you desire during your lifetime and can will them in any way you see fit. In other words, I have no legal claim to anything that is yours unless you choose to give it to me. Now do you understand?"

"You said you loved me," Jenny whispered in reply.

"What?"

"You said you loved me."

"So? What's new about that?"

"Oh, nothing," said Jenny.

"Do you love *me*, Jenny?"

With her head lowered, he could not see the tears shimmering in her eyes; he could only hear the teasing note in her voice. "Ask me when I'm not starving to death," Jenny said.

Chapter Twenty-seven

LORD DAVID ESCORTED JENNY TO WHAT HE had politely designated as the washroom. He half pushed the door open for her, and as she sailed past him, nose in air, offered a bit of information.

"There is no window, Jenny, and this is the only door. I shall stay well away at the end of the hallway to ensure your privacy, but I shall see you immediately you come out."

"Indeed?" said Jenny, as though it didn't matter in the least to her.

He grinned. "Indeed, yes, Jenny. Ah, here is Alice with some things you may need."

Alice was a short, round maid in black uniform and white apron. She was carrying a small tray of soap and toiletries and had two towels slung across her arm.

As she bobbed a curtsy and proceeded into the washroom, Jenny demanded excitedly of

Lord David, "Why didn't you tell me there was a maid here?"

"To help you run away?" he asked, staring intently into her face.

Jenny looked down, veiling her give-away eyes. "She could have helped me with my hooks and—and hair—and been company," she added, the pathetic note back in her voice.

"I am willing to let her do all that, Jenny, but I think I should warn you," he advised kindly, "that she will not help in any escape. She is one of *my* servants, and I have her promise. Besides which," his own dark eyes danced devilishly, "she does not think it right for you to try to run away with your married lover. Now, before you start to curse me," he said as he gave her a little push through the door, "send Alice out. Not being of the aristocracy, she is more easily shocked than you or I."

Her dinner that night consisted of the usual cup of tea and, instead of the single piece of toast, a buttered muffin Lord David proffered as though he were conferring the greatest of favors. Only her extreme state of hunger prevented Jenny from smashing it, butter side down, onto the top of his head.

"Would you like to play at cards when Ferguson and I return from the inn, Jenny?"

Jenny thought of the inn meal awaiting the

two men. She could almost smell the marvelous aroma of vegetable soup and baked chicken and potatoes roasted in their jackets. The vision of garden salad and sweet carrots and rice pudding was so vivid that she was ready to reach out—

"Jenny, are you all right?"

"Of course, I'm all right," she declared haughtily, walking about the little room to show him she was her usual vigorous self.

As soon as he was reassured, she realized she had made a mull of a wonderful opportunity. Well, there was always next time.

"Can Alice stay with me while you are gone?" she asked him.

He studied her suspiciously. "No."

"Oh, please, please, David." She clutched at him in pretended panic. "At least give her a key to hold."

"Why?"

"If anything should happen while you're gone," she whispered in apparent terror. "If there should be a fire—" She shuddered. "I would be trapped in here alone."

Seeing him weaken, she clutched at his arm again. "I promise I will not try to step foot out of this room while you are gone. Just let her be near with the key so I won't feel as though I'm in prison."

"All right. I'll do that," he said gruffly.

"Oh, thank you, David." She gave him a weak smile of mixed relief and gratitude, then covered her mouth to hold back a laugh as soon as he left her. She would warrant that the Earl of Denby's evening meal at the inn would sit as badly on his stomach later as his present state of conscience did right now.

She waited at her window eagerly for the sound of horses to die away in the distance, then shouted lustily, "Alice, Alice."

After five minutes, Alice came to the door.

"What is it, ma'am? I promised the master not to let you out."

"I don't want to get out. I want to speak to you. Please come in. I'll sit on the bed away from the door. You can hear it creak."

Alice unlocked the door, poked in her head to make sure the master's unwilling guest was still on the bed, and stood in the doorway.

"Yes, mum?"

Jenny held out a narrow gold bracelet set with small pearls and sapphires on one side and engraved with delicate scrollwork on the other.

"I want to give this to you."

Alice eyed the bracelet with covetous eyes. She wet her lips, then sighed and shook her head. "I promised my lord not to help you get away."

"No, no, you don't understand. I'll give it to

you in exchange for a meal. You didn't promise Lord David not to feed me, did you?" she asked cunningly. "Where's the harm in that? One meal for this lovely bracelet. Look at it—the jewels are real."

Drawn by cupidity, Alice drew closer, and Jenny was presently able to press the pretty bauble into her willing upturned palm.

"There's not much in the kitchen, just breakfast fixings."

"Breakfast fixings will be fine," Jenny declared fervently. "Lots of them. Just hurry, Alice."

Half an hour later, while Alice perched gingerly on the chair, abashed to be sitting in the presence of a lady, Jenny occupied the bed, her legs crossed under her as she feasted on three fried eggs, a thick chunk of ham, sliced tomatoes, two pieces of bread, and the heel of the loaf as well, all lavishly covered with both butter and strawberry jam, the whole washed down with three mugs of strong China tea.

When not a crumb remained, Jenny gave a sigh of repletion and lifted the tray off her lap to hold it out to Alice.

"There, take it away, and thank you, Alice. If you feed me as well tomorrow—morning and evening both," she stipulated cannily, "there will be a gold necklace in it for you."

An hour later when Lord David entered the room to bring her to the card table, Jenny lay on top of the coverings in the most seductive nightgown Peggy had included with her clothes—a sheer, white silk chiffon with a matching tulle-trimmed negligee.

Her head was on the pillow with her hair spread out in casual, careful disarray. The flowing skirt of her negligee had been purposefully pulled open, exposing bare feet and ankles and the bewitching silk-clad outline of limbs and thighs. Exaggerated sighing breaths stirred the lace over her bosom in exquisite rhythmic motions.

Lord David gulped and tried to avert his glance but found that his eyes had taken on a will of their own.

"Jenny, the card table is set up," he told her hoarsely.

"I think—not tonight, David." She smiled wanly. "I'm too—" She made as if to rise and fell back against the pillows. "Tired, so tired," she murmured pitifully.

Lord David's hands clenched against his sides.

"Would—would you like a cup of tea?"

"That would be nice," said Jenny in the same vague, failing voice.

When he brought her the tea ten minutes later, she was standing at the window, the negligee tied in front and her hair falling forward over her breast.

As he closed the door behind him, she took a step toward him, put a trembling hand to her head, and fell over in a heap at his feet.

Lying gracefully—she hoped—on the floor, Jenny tried not to wince as the cup and saucer fell to the floor, too, and hot tea splashed through the silk of her nightgown.

"Jenny, Jenny, my darling, my beloved, oh, my God, Jenny, open your eyes." He was on the floor, holding her in his arms. She was being held, shaken, hugged, kissed, and exhorted all at the same time.

Unwilling to prolong such agony, with a studied seductive play of her long lashes, Jenny obeyed the injunction to open her eyes.

Lord David drew her upright.

"You win, Jenny," he told her.

"W-win?"

"What kind of monster do you think I am?" he asked her roughly. "Yes, you win." He pulled a piece of paper out of his pocket and threw it onto the small chest of drawers. "That's the special license. I wanted to marry you more than anything in the world, but I'll take you any way I can get you. All right, Jenny. As of now, you're my mistress."

"I—I am?"

"Yes. I'll send Ferguson away first thing in

the morning and Alice, too. Shall you mind," he said as he took her hand tenderly, "beginning our life together here? Just the two of us alone?"

"It sounds fine," said Jenny weakly. Genuinely weakly this time.

"Just a minute."

He strode out of the room and was back a few minutes later.

"Alice will be up in a minute with a tray for you. There isn't much. Some eggs and ham, fried potatoes, bread, a little cheese. Will that be enough for you?" he asked anxiously.

When the tray was brought by a puzzled-looking Alice twenty minutes later, Jenny looked at it and barely kept from retching. David sat her in the wicker chair and stood over her, watching every single morsel that went into her mouth, urging her to eat more.

One single bite more, Jenny decided finally, and she was liable to faint in earnest.

"I think my stomach has shrunk," she insisted as she put the tray aside.

David took it from her and put it outside the door. He came back and locked the door from the inside.

"Now?" uttered poor Jenny, struggling against nausea.

"If you were my bride, Jenny—" He let his voice trail off and the implication speak for itself. "But with a mistress," he mentioned, poker-faced, "one doesn't buy a pig in the poke. I would like to see what I am getting."

"I suppose that's reasonable," Jenny agreed thoughtfully.

She untied the big tulle bow at the neck of her negligee and started wriggling out of the sleeves, pausing halfway through.

"Well, David?" she said.

"Well what?"

"Just that I would like to see what I am getting, too," Jenny told him gently. "Why should I, any more than you, buy a pig in the poke?"

The Earl of Denby's face went from the gray-white of shock to a rich blood-red. He eyed her grimly for a moment, then shrugged matter-of-factly and, while Jenny watched with interest, removed his jacket and waistcoat.

Off came Lady Melville's negligee, to be flung on the bed, while Lord David unbuttoned his fine lawn shirt.

Then they looked at each other, and both took one quick step forward. They both spoke together.

"You're wearing my pearls."

"You're wearing my locket."

"I never stopped."

"I always do."

They were in each other's arms, and Jenny was weeping, with her face against his bare chest, his hair tickling her nose and chin and getting in her eyes. He clutched her shoulders through the thin silk of her gown. "My darling girl, I love you so, I have always loved you. When you came home after your mother died, I was still too full of hurt pride and anger to admit it. I had to play the fool and flirt and show you there were others to whom I was a desirable husband."

He lifted up her wet, swollen face. "I came after you the very next day, as you told me three days ago that you once came after me. You were already gone. On a visit to your sister Margaret's, your father said. I went to her home, but you never arrived. So I returned to Somerset to start the search all over again, only to learn that you had married Sir Charles Melville."

"Because I thought you didn't want me any more," Jenny was sobbing again into the hairy chest, "and I needed someone to take care of me."

"I never knew anyone so capable of taking care of herself as you, Jenny, but I do think you need someone permanent in your life to love. I know I do. I need your love, Jenny. Desperately. I need you."

Jenny lifted her head and, with her finger-

tips, brushed some tendrils of his hair off her
face and tongue.

"Well, why in damnation didn't you say so a
long time ago," she asked him indignantly,
"instead of all that nonsense about children
and a country home in which to leave me
while you went off to Liverpool and London?"

"I said what I thought you wanted to hear,
Jenny. I wanted you to know that I would
never clip your wings."

"I thought you meant *I* would stay home
with the children and *you* would be free to
cavort in Liverpool with Sheila Dale and all
your other mistresses."

"All my other mistresses? I don't think I'm
nearly as virile as you give me credit for, my
love."

"You had better be," said Jenny unblushing-
ly, looking him straight in the eye. "I have
waited a long time. I want it to have been for
something worthwhile."

"I can only do my best," grinned the earl,
going over to the chest and picking up the
special license.

"Shall I send Ferguson for the vicar,
Jenny?"

"Of course." She tossed her hair back arro-
gantly. "I always intended for you to—once
you admitted you loved me."

"I realized that," he said amiably, "once I

had tasted the ham and eggs on your breath when I kissed you after your supposed faint."

Jenny pushed him away in exasperation. "Oh, you bastard!" Then she burst out laughing. "You bloody bastard," she amended adoringly.

Chapter Twenty-eight

THE ROOMS OF THE EARL AND COUNTESS AT Denby House had been recently done over, combining them into one large apartment consisting of a huge bedroom, a sitting room, and two small, separate dressing rooms.

"I believe a husband and wife should sleep side by side," Lord David told his bride. "That way it will be easier to obey the vicar and not let the sun go down on our quarrels."

"We don't *have* to quarrel," suggested Jenny provocatively.

"And fish don't have to swim, and birds don't have to fly," retorted Lord David.

Jenny was poking about her new quarters.

"Where does this door lead to?"

Her husband of four hours did not answer. Jenny looked around at him questioningly and saw that he was smiling a disturbing kind of smile.

She pushed open the door.

It was just a small chamber and contained only one piece of furniture—a large, battered old desk.

Lord David came up behind her. His arms went around her, his hands crossing in front over her breasts. He kissed her behind the ears. "I had it shipped from Liverpool after the shareholders' meeting," he whispered. "It seemed to inspire you so."

He started to unbutton the half-dozen tiny buttons at the front of her jacket, then turned her around and began unhooking the dozen hooks at the back of her dress.

When she was standing before him with no other covering than a chemise and her foxfire hair, "Shall we try our desk, Jenny?" he asked her huskily.

"Tomorrow."

"Tomorrow?"

"It's a long story," said Jenny. "I'll be glad to explain why tonight I think a bed would be—"

"More comfortable?"

"That, too," Jenny admitted, "though the word I had in mind was—er—suitable."

"Suitable?"

"For my deflowering."

"Your—"

"I'm a virgin," Jenny said apologetically.

"Good God!"

"I know it's a bit of a shock to you," sympathized Jenny. "You see, it was this way—"

"Shut up, Jenny!" he told her pleasantly.

"I beg your pardon?"

He scooped her up in his arms. "No more talking, I beg you. There has been more than enough already. Tomorrow you can tell me all about it in the greatest detail. Right now I propose, without any conversation, to end your distressing state of chastity." He dumped her onto the enormous Queen Anne bed. "If you have no objections?"

Jenny lifted the chemise over her head and tossed it onto the floor. She lay back on the bed, naked and smiling, and carefully spread her hair out over the pillow. "No," said Jenny with dignity, "no objections at all."

Tapestry

HISTORICAL ROMANCES

Breathtaking New Tales

of love and adventure set against history's most exciting time and places. Featuring two novels by the finest authors in the field of romantic fiction—every month.

Next Month From Tapestry Romances

LADY RAINE
by Carol Jerina
LAND OF GOLD
by Mary Ann Hammond

If you enjoyed the passion and adventure of this book...

then you're sure to enjoy the Tapestry Home Subscription Service℠!

You'll receive two new Tapestry™ romance novels each month, as soon as they are published, delivered right to your door.

Examine your books for 15 days, free...

Return the coupon below, and we'll send you two Tapestry romances to examine for 15 days, free. If you're as thrilled with your books as we think you will be, just pay the enclosed invoice. Then every month, you'll receive two intriguing Tapestry love stories—and you'll never pay any postage, handling, or packing costs. If not delighted, simply return the books and owe nothing. There is no minimum number of books to buy, and you may cancel at any time.

Return the coupon today . . . and soon you'll enjoy all the love, passion and adventure of times gone by!

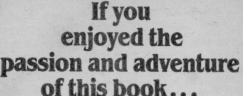

HISTORICAL *Tapestry* ROMANCES

**Tapestry Home Subscription Service, Dept. RPSR 12
120 Brighton Road, Box 5020, Clifton, N.J. 07015**

Yes, I'd like to receive 2 exciting Tapestry historical romances each month as soon as they are published. The books are mine to examine for 15 days, free. If I decide to keep the books, I will pay only $2.50 each, a total of $5.00. If not delighted, I can return them and owe nothing. There is never a charge for this convenient home delivery—no postage, handling, or any other hidden charges. **I understand there is no minimum number of books I must buy, and that I can cancel this arrangement at any time.**

☐ Mrs. ☐ Miss ☐ Ms. ☐ Mr.

Name	(please print)

Address	Apt. #

City ( )	State	Zip

Area Code	Telephone Number

Signature (if under 18, parent or guardian must sign)

This offer, limited to one per household, expires September 30, 1984. Terms and prices subject to change. Your enrollment is subject to acceptance by Simon & Schuster Enterprises.

Tapestry™ is a trademark of Simon & Schuster, Inc.